Christine Merrill lives on a farm in Wisconsin, USA, with her husband, two sons and too many pets—all of whom would like her to get off the computer so they can check their e-mail. She has worked by turns in theatre costuming and as a librarian. Writing historical romance combines her love of good stories and fancy dress with her ability to stare out of the window and make stuff up.

A SCANDALOUS MATCH FOR THE MARQUESS

Christine Merrill

MILLS & BOON

First published in Great Britain 2024
by Mills & Boon, an imprint of HarperCollins*Publishers* Ltd,
1 London Bridge Street, London, SE1 9GF

www.harpercollins.co.uk

HarperCollins*Publishers*, Macken House, 39/40 Mayor Street Upper,
Dublin 1, D01 C9W8, Ireland

ISBN: 978-0-263-32078-7

07/24

To Megan Haslam: onward and upward.

Chapter One

Felicity Morgan had never planned to be a disgrace.

When she'd had her come-out, five years ago, her mother had warned of the weakening effect that champagne and moonlight might have on a girl's resolve, and she took them both in moderation. Likewise, she did not put too much stock in the compliments of gentleman, and none at all in the suggestions of rakes.

In many ways Felicity was a very sensible girl. But in others she kept her head firmly in the clouds.

When men spoke to her, they often came away thinking that she had no interest in hearing what they had to say. It was not scepticism or boredom. Just a lack of interest, as if she was listening to another conversation more fascinating than anything they could offer. She seemed just as happy to be sitting alone at the side of the room as she was when someone paid court to her and was unwilling or unable to share her attention with any one gentleman long enough to earn a proposal from him.

There was nothing wrong with her looks. She had fine eyes, a sweet smile and an enviable figure. Nor was her dress out of step with the current fashion. Her parents provided a generous allowance to outfit her in new designs, year after year.

But the Seasons had passed without a proposal of any kind. Her father was losing patience and her own mother hinted that a bit of scandal might do her some good. If she unbent a trifle and allowed some small lapses in judgement it might give the fellows encouragement.

It was clear that if something did not change she was headed for genteel spinsterhood. In her opinion that was no bad thing. It was not that she didn't like men. As a group, she found them fascinating, mysterious, and alien in their thoughts and actions. She wanted to study them from a safe distance.

But after watching her parents together Felicity had come to believe that marriage was no guarantee of happiness. Her father was a demanding man with a short temper. With her attempts to placate him her mother seemed to grow smaller and quieter and more miserable with each passing year.

But many unmarried ladies of her acquaintance seemed quite content with their lot. They had friends and interests and were, overall, happier than their married sisters. There was no reason to think that she would not be the same if everyone would give up on the idea of her marrying and leave her alone with her thoughts.

For she did have thoughts. Plans, as well. With the implementation of them her future would be sorted and a successful and happy life alone all but guaranteed. If she could have kept her intentions a secret from her parents for just a few more months she'd have earned enough to set up housekeeping on her own and could have lived quite comfortably for the rest of her life.

But it was not to be. Her parents had discovered her secret and declared it so scandalous, so horrifying, so far out of bounds as to render her a public embarrassment. Her mother had wept, and her father had confiscated the money she'd saved for the future. Then he had announced that she was banished from his house. She was not to set foot in London until she came to her senses, or until a suitable man could be found to marry her and mould her into the docile and obedient woman society expected her to be.

The second prospect was highly unlikely. They had already established that no one in town wanted her. Now they were sending her to Shropshire to stay with a friend of her grandmother, the widowed sister of a duke. Felicity doubted that husbands lay thick on the ground in the village of Vicar's Hill, even if her infamy had not carried that far.

Of course, the chances were even worse that she would come to her senses.

She smiled at the thought. Her father might disagree, but there was nothing nonsensical about her aspirations. Once she was out of sight of her parents she would carry on as she had been doing. If her chaperon, Lady Ophelia Winterbottom, could be persuaded to give her a trifle more freedom than she'd had in London she might continue to do just as she wished. If not then she would simply have to find a way around the old woman. But in the end she would have her way.

The long and bumpy ride on the mail coach from London, which her father had said would curb her stubbornness, had only strengthened her resolve. If she ever meant to get out from under the collective thumb of her family she would not allow herself to be contained or curtailed or transformed from a downtrodden girl into a resigned woman. She would break free.

She would view this trip as an adventure and a chance to reinvent herself as the independent spirit she wanted to be. Travel was supposed to broaden the mind. A trip to a remote English village was not the same as floating down a canal in Venice. But it was better than nothing.

And it would all begin in a few miles, when she reached her destination.

She stared out through the coach window and ahead, eyes firmly fixed on the horizon and the bright future that she was sure lay beyond it.

Without warning, the carriage stopped. And when she looked at where she actually was her hopes fell. The countryside where they were sitting did not look like a bright future. It looked identical to the last dozen empty miles. There was no quaint town full of cheerful people to welcome her. There was nothing at all.

'Vicar's Hill,' the driver called over the jingling of harnesses and the stamping of horses impatient to get on their way.

'Are you sure?' she said doubtfully, staring out of the window at the empty road around them and off towards a horizon that held nothing but trees. 'I do not see a village.'

'Vicar's Hill corner,' the driver corrected, taking her bags down from the top of the coach and dropping them at the side of the road. 'That is as close as we come.'

Then he dropped a small mail bag next to the

stone mile marker and stared at her expectantly, waiting for her to exit the coach and join her luggage.

'There is supposed to be someone to meet me,' she said, refusing to budge. 'They are not here yet.'

'That is none of my concern,' he said, opening the door and gesturing to the muddy road.

She had expected a carriage, or a wagon, driven by a ruddy-cheeked servant of kindly old Ophelia to greet her and help her to the house. But, as it so often did, her imagination did not correspond with the facts.

'What am I to do?' she asked, staring off into the distance and then back to the coachman.

'Wait,' he suggested. 'Or walk. Your choice, miss.'

She got down from the carriage, her travelling boots squelching as she stepped onto the wet earth of the road. 'Is there a house?' she asked. 'A village? A farm of some kind where I can ask for assistance?'

There had to be a sign of civilisation somewhere near, else he wouldn't have stopped.

He shrugged and gestured up the road. 'Whatever there is lies that way.'

She glanced at her baggage, which sat in a pile beside the road, looking as forlorn as she felt.

Without waiting for an answer he took his seat again, reaching for the reins to signal the horses.

'You can't just leave me here,' she said, staring up at him.

'I am sorry, miss,' he said as the horses started off. 'I've a schedule to keep. Someone will come along in time to get the mail, I'm sure. They'll take care of you as well.'

And then he was rolling away, the wheels of the coach splattering her with mud as he left her behind.

She stared up the road until the horses and carriage disappeared around a bend. Then she looked around her at the T-shaped junction she'd been abandoned on, and the sack of mail that ranked ahead of her in importance to the villagers. How long would it be before someone came for it? And what was she to do in the meantime?

There was no point in going back, for she'd been there already, and no point in going forward, for the driver would have let her out farther down the road if that was her direction.

The only choice was the road to the left, which must be the way to the village. She sat on her trunks and waited for nearly half an hour, hoping that the problem would solve itself. Then she gave up and set off walking, leaving all but a small valise behind to be collected by the servants once she had made someone aware of her presence.

After a mile, her skirts and shoes were heavy with

mud, and she seemed no closer to her destination than she had been. There was no change in the scenery. The countryside rolled out on either side of her as far as she could see. She was tired and thirsty and regretting the one case she had chosen to carry, which seemed to grow heavier with each step.

It was bad enough that she had been banished from London and exiled to this distant spot, expected to repent of her misdeeds. The least Lady Ophelia could have done was to send someone for her. She had not expected to be treated as if she did not matter at all.

She stopped and sat on her bag to rest and contemplated tears. She had not cried thus far, even when Father had shouted at her. Crying would not have made him relent, nor would he have believed her tears a sign of repentance.

They would not do her any good now, either. They would leave her more parched than she already was, and they really did not fit her current mood. She was not so much sad as she was annoyed by this latest turn of events.

What she had wanted to do, from the very start, was to scream at the injustice of it all. If she had been a man, or even a boy, the strictures of society would not have been as rigid and no one would have thought twice about what she had done. Some might have even considered it an achievement.

But because she was a girl her parents had thought it scandalous and sent her away. And now here she was, alone. She got up, ready to stomp off towards the village in disgust, only to find that her feet were sunk deep in a muddy rut. As she pulled them free she lost first one shoe and then the other, leaving her stocking-footed in the puddle.

It was all too much—the final straw to break the back of her burdened patience. She opened her mouth, took in a great breath, and screamed out her rage and frustration into the empty countryside.

From a group of trees to her right there came a whirring of wings as a flock of birds took to the sky in alarm, followed by the solidly masculine sound of cursing. Then, as if from nowhere, a huge man loomed up out of the thicket and lurched towards her. By the scowl on his face, the set of his broad shoulders and the way he stomped as he walked, she could tell he was angry.

She sat down on her bag again, hurrying to empty her shoes of water and get them back on her feet in case she needed to run, keeping one eye on the man as he approached. He was dressed in worn leather breeches and the sort of loose, many-pocketed coat worn by gamekeepers or poachers. The straw hat he was wearing was missing a piece of its brim, as if a horse or some other large animal had taken a bite from it.

She had probably interrupted some nefarious behaviour with her scream. What other reason would this ruffian have to be alone in the middle of nowhere? And now he was enraged and coming to punish her in ways that she could hardly imagine.

But that did not stop her from trying, for she had an incredibly good imagination. She could already feel those large hands clasping her shoulders, shaking her into submission…

He would want her to submit to something, she was sure. Despite his rough clothing, he was a handsome brute in the rough way of literary villains, whose vices never seemed to show in their faces. Dark hair curled from beneath the unfortunate hat and equally dark eyes blazed from underneath his knitted brows. His sharp cheekbones were covered with a day's stubble that would make any forced kisses feel rough against a lady's soft skin. She shivered at the thought.

And now he was towering over her, hands on hips, as if waiting for an explanation.

'Hello,' she said cautiously, regretting her earlier outburst.

'What the devil are you doing here?' he said, raising one hand to shield his eyes from the sun to get a better look at her.

'I am looking for the dower house at Woodley Hall,' she said, clambering over the valise to keep it between them. 'I came on the mail coach. Someone was supposed to meet me, but they did not arrive.'

'You couldn't have,' he said firmly, denying the obvious. 'There is no coach on Tuesday.'

'It is Wednesday,' she said, equally firmly.

He counted on his fingers, muttering under his breath. 'Sunday mutton, Monday chicken, last night beef, which made it Tuesday.' He looked up at her, surprised. 'You are right. It is Wednesday. But you had no reason to scream about it and scare the birds.'

'I had every reason in the world,' she said. 'I do not give a fig for what the birds think—unless they can fly me out of this mud hole and back to London. Or perhaps they can get my luggage—which is still sitting at the junction with the mail…'

Her words faded away as she looked at him again, standing tall and threatening beside her. She should not have admitted where she'd come from, nor that she had left her baggage unguarded. If he was a poacher, as she suspected, he might now be thinking of rifling through her things for valuables.

But he made no move to do so. He was still staring at her and still annoyed. She took another step away.

'You still should not have screamed,' he said in a brusque tone. 'I was worried that someone was in true danger, not just being foolish.'

'I am not being foolish,' she insisted, though she did feel so now that he mentioned it. 'I was overcome with frustration. It has been a long and trying week.' Then she smiled hopefully. 'But if you could send to the house for someone to collect me and my things…?'

He was still frowning.

'Or perhaps you could simply tell me how much farther I must walk,' she said, giving up. 'And then I'll just be on my way, shall I? I won't bother you any further.'

Seconds ticked by and he stared at her in silence, probably wondering where to dispose of her body after he'd made an end of her. But then, just as she was preparing to run, she heard the sound of wagon wheels and the jingle of harnesses growing closer. A cart appeared around the next curve in the road.

'Miss Morgan!' the wagon driver called, speeding up as he saw her answering wave.

'Here!' she called, and stumbled up the road to meet him. When she arrived at the wagon's side she looked back at the stranger on the road. 'No need to bother. Someone has come to get me, after all.'

'If you are all right, then…' he said, as if he had

meant to help her all along. Then he glanced back towards the trees he had come from.

'Quite all right, thank you,' she replied, relieved that they were no longer alone together.

'I'll just be going back to my hide,' he replied, backing away from her.

'Be my guest,' she said, giving him a wary look as he disappeared back into the brush.

Before the servant could get down to help her she had climbed up into the safety of the wagon. As he apologised for the delay and prepared to collect her luggage, she stared at the retreating back of the mysterious man from the woods, wondering if she would see him again. Perhaps when she got to the dower house she could enquire about him and his odd behaviour. For, really, what else was there to do in the country but speculate about the neighbours?

If there was no story to be told then she would simply have to write her own.

She smiled as the driver set off towards the dower house, content that the fantasy version of her encounter would be even more interesting than the truth.

He had forgotten the day. Again.

Martin Howell sat in the little shed he'd erected, staring out through the slitted windows towards the road and the retreating wagon. It was Wednesday, and Aunt Ophelia had asked him to be at the crossroads an hour ago to greet Miss Morgan from London and escort her to the dower house. It was a simple request—the sort any idiot could have managed. And yet he had bungled it.

He had only meant to spend a little of his morning in the wild, gathering his thoughts. But, as it often did, time had got away from him. All of a sudden it had been half past two in the afternoon and he had not given a thought to the fact that the mail coach arrived at two, and he was on foot and in no condition to receive guests.

If she hadn't screamed he'd not have noticed her at all and she'd have been left to walk all the way to the house. But the bullfinch nest he had been observing had shown its first signs of activity and he'd been distracted. The female had left it for little more than an hour, and through his spyglass he had been able to see four tiny heads, beaks tipped to the sky, waiting for the mother's return.

He took another look now, and closed his eyes briefly to fix the image in his mind. Then he set the spyglass aside, took up a sketchbook and drew what he had seen with hurried strokes of his pencil. It was lucky that he had an excellent memory for such things. Drawing live birds was difficult, as they tended to hop around and take wing at the slightest disturbance.

Other naturalists resorted to snares and taxidermy if they wished to draw their subjects. But he did not see the point of killing a thing to study it better. He'd seen far too much of death to surround himself with it now.

Without meaning to, he increased his pressure on the pencil and the lead cracked, spoiling the line. He reached for a penknife to sharpen it again.

Really, it was lucky that the birds had come back at all after Miss Morgan's tantrum on the road. But none of that would have happened if he had been where he should have been at the appointed time.

His servants had remembered, even if he had not. Mrs Spang, the housekeeper, had probably sent the wagon to find her, hoping that the coach was late. Peters, the footman driving it, would have guessed his dilemma and taken the blame for his error. The staff knew his faults too well, and looked out for him when he got preoccupied and forgot things.

Aunt Ophelia would hear of his absence and make apologies for him as well. She had to do that far too often. He must get hold of himself...

He gathered up the spyglass and sketchbook and put them in the rucksack he'd brought, along with the remains of his lunch. Then he set off towards the main house to try to make amends for his careless-ness. It was disconcerting, this feeling of being un-tethered from time, having to distinguish its passing by remembering the evening meals, which did not vary from week to week.

That was another thing which he supposed should worry him. It probably bored the cook, preparing the same seven meals over and over again. But not as much as approving any change bothered him. When the staff had first come to him with the task he had taken one look at the final menu penned by his dear Emma, which had still been sitting on the morning room desk, and had lacked the heart to replace it. Three years later it remained there, a perpetual re-minder that the house no longer had a mistress.

If he could not manage his own life, what was he supposed to do with Miss Morgan? Technically, she was under Aunt Ophelia's care, and not his. But he was the head of the family here, and Ophelia would expect him to put on a cravat and a proper coat and welcome her to the property at dinner tonight.

He hoped he would not be expected to entertain her further. He had not heard what she had done to get herself sent down from London, but after seeing her he had his suspicions. She was a comely thing, with tendrils of shiny dark hair escaping from under her bonnet. She had large, dark eyes, and a very kissable mouth. A face like that could be a man's undoing...

If she was here and not on her way to the altar, the man had not been the one to come undone. He hoped Ophelia was up to the task of keeping the girl in line until a proper husband could be found for her. Or until the results of her indiscretion could be delivered and handed over to some farmer or villager to be raised quietly.

Such discreet births happened often enough, he was sure. Just never on his property. The fact that one of his tenants might be forced to raise her mistake was annoying. There had been nothing repentant about her when he had met her just now. She'd treated him as though she were his better, not someone in disgrace and dependent on his charity to minimise her shame.

But it was rather judgmental of him to ascribe all the blame to her. More than enough of it lay with the sort of men who sowed wild oats with abandon, taking advantage of proper young ladies who were often raised ignorant of where a dalliance might lead and of how hard it was to resist, once passions were inflamed.

His own wife, God rest her soul, had proved to him that women had urges, much the same as men had. Was it really justice to punish this girl for succumbing to her desires, when the man leading her to temptation had got off scot-free?

It was even possible that she had been promised marriage, only to be abandoned when her pursuer had got what he wanted from her. If this was the truth he felt more sympathy, for he knew what it was to be young and in love and to be bitterly disappointed when life did not turn out as planned.

He had arrived at the hall now, and put the thought to the back of his mind as he kicked the dirt from his boots. Then he walked in through the front door, hazarding a glance in the long mirror of the main hall and wincing at his own appearance.

He looked like a bumpkin. No wonder Miss Morgan had treated him as she had. She had probably assumed he was some sort of vagrant, living rough on the estate.

And he had done nothing to dissuade such thoughts, arguing the days of the week with her and forgetting to make a proper introduction. He had been spending so much time alone with his own thoughts that he was incapable of holding a civil conversation.

He rubbed his unshaven cheek. Standards had grown slack in the three years since he had left the city, but his current state of dishevelment was unsatisfactory, even for him. He would likely be expected at Ophelia's for supper, where he must apologise for his earlier behaviour. It was too much to hope that Miss Morgan would not recognise him as the man she had met on the road. But after a bath and a shave she might at least think that rough fellow had been an aberration and not his true self.

With that plan in place, he started up the stairs to his rooms, ready to make amends.

Chapter Two

Felicity sat in silence on the boards of the wagon seat as the driver went back to the junction to re-trieve her trunks and then turned off the road, trav-elling almost two miles before reaching the dower house on the Woodley estate. As they passed the place where she'd finally been picked up there was no sign of the strange man she'd spoken with.

He'd said he was going back to his 'hide', which had made no sense to her. She supposed that it must be some sort of shack or hovel where he lived. But what or who was he hiding from? She must remem-ber, if she came this way again, to bring a maid or a footman, since it was clearly not safe to be wander-ing these country roads alone.

Perhaps in the future she could borrow a pony cart or a small carriage to make her way around. But if the estate had such a thing, why hadn't they sent it to get her now? The rough vehicle she was currently riding in made her feel like another piece of luggage, to be towed to its destination and forgotten again.

It did not bode well for the welcome she was likely to get when she arrived at the house. Perhaps the whole place was an unkempt ruin.

Her imagination ran on ahead of her, picturing the gothic monstrosity she was to be housed in and the mysterious woman who lived there.

But then they turned up the drive and she saw the actual dower house, and her fears eased. It was not the ramshackle place she'd feared, but built of white stone with a path bordered by roses, clean windows sparkling in the afternoon sun, and a solid slate roof to keep out the weather.

Lady Ophelia was waiting in the doorway, a worried expression on her face. She was a tall woman with a pleasant manner, her white hair piled high under an equally white lace cap.

'Oh, dear. Oh, my dear,' she said, holding out her hands in an apologetic welcome. 'This was not how you were supposed to arrive at all. Martin was to come for you.' She paused in her apology to look Felicity over from head to toe, taking in her muddy skirts and flushed face. 'You are Miss Morgan, aren't you? And you appear to have had an adventure. Oh, dear.'

'Nothing that cannot be recovered from,' she said,

giving what she hoped was a game smile. 'And you must be Lady Ophelia,' she added, when no introduction seemed forthcoming.

'Of course,' the older woman replied with an embarrassed nod. 'You must think us all without manners to greet you in such a way. Come into the house and rest yourself. There is tea laid in the parlour. Lemonade and cakes as well. I am sure you are tired and hungry after your journey.'

The words flooded out of the woman in a rush as she ushered Felicity inside.

'My shoes,' Felicity said, staring down at the mud drying on the leather. 'I look a state.'

'Do not worry yourself about it,' Ophelia said as they seated themselves in the parlour. 'You cannot be blamed for the vagaries of travel. My nephew was supposed to come for you, but the poor boy is so absent-minded it is apparent that he forgot.'

'That is all right,' she said, hiding her annoyance behind a polite smile.

And perhaps this inauspicious beginning was not the disaster it appeared. If the whole family was scatter-brained they might forget that she was here as a punishment and let her do as she pleased.

'When you did not appear I was so worried,' Ophelia said. 'I sent a servant to the main house, to remind

Martin of your arrival and to invite him to dine with us this evening.'

'That sounds delightful,' she said, quietly wishing this Martin person to the devil and wondering if she should mention the stranger in the woods. She decided against it. The servant had seen him and said nothing about his presence. Perhaps he was the gamekeeper and as dotty as everyone else she'd met here.

'Martin is Marquess of Woodley,' Lady Ophelia replied with an encouraging smile. 'The first son of my brother the Duke. And single as well.' She followed this with a wink, to make the hint even more obvious.

Felicity was unsure how to respond, since she was not in the market for a husband. Was she supposed to be entertaining fantasies of marrying the heir to a dukedom before she'd even brushed the dust of travel from her gown?

After an awkward pause, she said, 'I look forward to meeting him.'

Several hours too late, she added to herself, and sipped her lemonade.

Then she glanced at the writing desk in the corner and felt her pulse quicken. 'But before dinner I must write to my parents, to assure them that I have arrived safely.'

'Of course, my dear,' Ophelia said with a benevolent nod.

She stood and went to the desk, pulling a little gold key from a chain around her neck and setting out a fresh quill and a single sheet of white paper from the small stack in the desk drawer before locking the desk again and gesturing to Felicity.

Felicity stared at the paper, confused.

'Your father was very specific in his instructions for your stay here. No more than one letter a day,' the old woman said with a sad nod. 'And one sheet should be sufficient. If I am honest, not much happens here that is worth writing about.'

'I see,' Felicity replied, carefully hiding her frustration.

Her parents intended this to be an incarceration, not a holiday, and Lady Ophelia was not so addled as to have missed the truth of that.

'Perhaps, if you would show me my room, I will write it later.'

'Of course,' Lady Ophelia said with an understanding nod. Then she set her teacup aside and rose, gesturing to the door. 'Mary, the maid, will have unpacked your things by now, and she can help you change. Dinner is at seven. We keep early hours in the country.'

'I will prepare myself,' Felicity said, and followed her hostess dutifully out of the room.

Martin arrived at the dower house promptly at half past six, ready to make up for his earlier lapse by being both present and early. The new addition to the household was nowhere to be seen, but his aunt was waiting for him in the sitting room, already dressed for dinner.

'Martin,' she said, with a resigned tone and an equally frustrated expression.

Then she looked him up and down, inspecting his coat and noting the fresh shave and haircut before sagging in relief.

'Did you think I was likely to shame you by coming in my birding coat?' he asked, giving her an encouraging smile.

'Well, you did forget the day,' she reminded him. 'I was unsure what you were likely to do next.'

'Fair enough,' he agreed. 'But I am attempting to make things right again, so you needn't worry.'

'Better late than never, I suppose. And you would do well to behave yourself. The girl is quite charming and might prove to be excellent company.'

'So she made it here all right,' he said, consoling himself over his earlier lapse.

'She is not at all what I expected,' Ophelia said with a smile.

'And just what were you expecting?' he asked with a frown.

She shook her head, as if keeping a secret. 'Let us say there is no sign of scandal about her, and nor has her spirit been crushed by this sudden fall from grace.'

'Maybe it should have been,' he said automatically.

'Really, Martin. You did used not to be so prim.'

Perhaps that was true. He could hardly remember what he had been in the past. 'In any case, she is no concern of mine.'

'She has at least concerned you enough that you have bothered to shave.' Ophelia gave him another appraising look. 'That is more than you are usually willing to do for me when we dine together.'

'It was time,' he said with a shrug.

'Or perhaps you are simply waking up from a long slumber,' she said with another encouraging smile. 'She is pretty. Very pretty indeed.'

'That is also no concern of mine,' he muttered.

It was true, though. She was quite handsome. Different from the sort of woman he favoured, of course. Emma had been ethereal, with blonde hair and skin like porcelain. Miss Morgan was earthly in a most disquieting way.

'What did she do to get herself banished from London?' he asked, to break the train of thought.

He should show some interest in the sort of people his aunt was associating with, if only to show concern for her welfare.

'Now, that is truly none of your business,' Ophelia said with a sly smile. 'If she is to make a fresh start, she must leave such problems behind. And so must we. The last thing she needs in her current friendless state is to have her tablemates judging her morals over dinner.'

'Very well,' he said, not satisfied with the answer.

Aunt Ophelia's obfuscation did not really matter. He'd suspected the truth about Miss Morgan when he'd looked at her lips, which were red and kissable. Someone had taken liberties there, he was sure.

'But if she gets into further trouble while she's here I recommend you send her straight back to where she came from.'

He'd felt uneasy when he looked at her, as if he was looking at a storm on the horizon.

'Nonsense,' Ophelia replied, giving him a stern look. 'For one thing, I fail to see what trouble she could possibly get into in Vicar's Hill. I have spent enough time in the area to assure you that even if you were to stir yourself from that hovel you keep in the marsh you would find there is no mischief to be had.'

'And for another?' he added.

'For another, her presence here is a good thing. For both of us,' she added, giving him another speculative look.

'I do not need company,' he said, giving her a sharp look in return. 'My life is fine just the way it is.'

Or at least it had been before he'd met Miss Morgan. Now he felt disorientated and confused.

His aunt was looking at him in disbelief. 'When your father dies you will take his title and his place in Parliament. You will have to marry and beget an heir. Unless you are telling me that you mean to forsake everything he stands for?'

He shook his head, denying the obvious. 'He is in perfect health. There is no reason to think that I will outlive him.'

'Other than common sense,' she replied. 'Unless you have plans to end your life before it has run its course.'

Now she was giving him a probing look, as if she could root the truth out of him with a glance.

He did not want to worry her by telling her that such dark thoughts occasionally troubled him. Not as often as they had after Emma's death, thank God.

Then, the black moods that had come upon him had not lifted for days at a time. Now he only had fleeting moments, when the rain came and he could not get outside to walk the fields, when he felt there was no point in going on.

'That was the moment when you were to assure me that I was wrong,' she said with a disapproving shake of her head.

'I have an occupation,' he said, gesturing towards the window and all the wild lands beyond it. 'I keep busy. I have no interest in Parliament or in putting an end to myself. Or in marrying again,' he added.

Especially not to the first woman he'd happened upon on the road, no matter how attractive she might be.

'It is good that you have your book to work on,' his aunt said cautiously. 'A thorough cataloguing of the birds of the area has never been done, and your sketches are really quite lovely.'

'I mean to improve on Bewick's guide by adding colour plates,' he said. 'But if I am to do justice to the living subjects it will take much study.'

'I am aware of that,' she replied. 'But there is nothing about the completion of that task that requires you to be unmarried.'

He laughed. 'If you intend me to take on Miss Morgan, you must be grasping at straws. You have known her for only a few hours, and I doubt she is as taken with this visit as you are.'

'What do you mean by that?' Ophelia asked.

'She does not want to be here,' he replied bluntly. 'She would not have come to the area without being forced to.'

'And you have so great a love of the village that you refuse to leave?' Ophelia responded. 'There are birds in London, after all. And in Norfolk, where your father lives. You do not have to reside here.'

And yet this was where he had come with Emma when they'd married, and he could not seem to leave it.

'I am happy here,' he lied, and then amended that to, 'Content.'

Now his aunt was looking at him with disappointment, as she had when he had first come into the room. 'I had hoped for so much more for you than contentment.'

'As had I,' he admitted with a sigh. 'But now it is enough. I do not mean to spoil my current peace by flirting with some wayward girl from London.'

At the doorway there was a faint clearing of a throat, and he looked up to see Miss Morgan, who had probably heard his last statement. Once again, he had embarrassed himself in front of her.

Or perhaps not. She was staring at him as if she

was too shocked to care about his words. 'You...' she said, pointing at him.

'Miss Felicity Morgan, may I present the Marquess of Woodley?' Ophelia said, then glared at Martin. 'But it appears that you have already met.'

'On the road today,' Miss Morgan said, her finger shaking to emphasise each word. 'I thought you were...'

'A tramp,' Ophelia finished for her. Then she turned to Martin. 'Tell me you were not wearing that horrible poacher's coat.'

He shrugged in response, then turned back to the girl and attempted a smile. 'Miss Morgan, I have come to apologise for my neglect of you this afternoon. And for my lack of an introduction. I was distracted.'

'I understand,' she said, her face trying to settle on an expression that could cover both confusion and irritation.

Then the long-case clock in the hall struck seven, and Ophelia interrupted. 'Martin, why don't you escort Miss Morgan to the dining room?' She added another significant look, in case either of them was still unaware of her efforts to matchmake.

'I don't think that will be...'

'Of course.'

They spoke in unison, but he was the louder of

the two, drowning out her objection and offering his arm.

She looked up at him with a smile that did not quite meet her eyes and allowed herself to be led in to dinner.

While Ophelia took the head of the table, Felicity was seated directly across from the Marquess. It gave her no choice but to look at him each time she raised her eyes from her plate. Not that she wished to. After his overheard comment about her being a wayward girl, she had no more desire to flirt with him than he did her.

She had not known his opinion before meeting him. At Ophelia's recommendation she had dressed for dinner with as much care as she would have in London, as if it was important to make a good impression on the titled stranger. Now he probably thought she was angling for a husband.

In truth, she was just tired of being thought a quiz. If she was to be a spinster, she wanted to acquire an air of mystery. She was making a new start here in Shropshire, and she would rather he thought her a beautiful stranger with a scandalous past than someone whose better days were behind her.

It was some consolation to think that he had decided the same thing when preparing to meet her.

The unfortunate straw hat and poacher's coat had been replaced by a fresh haircut and a superfine coat that was as well cut as anything she'd seen in London. His athletic build, which had seemed menacing when she'd met him in the field, now looked masterful. His stubbled chin had been shaved clean.

To claim he was not handsome would be a lie. If she'd been the sort of girl who sighed over unattainable men she might well have sighed over this one. His brown eyes alone were enough to make the breath catch in her throat.

But she must not let her head be turned by his good looks. He was not a proper marquess at all, since he was living as far removed from London as she was herself. She wondered what he had done to end up here during the Season, instead of enjoying society with the rest of the *ton*. Did his father think him a disgrace as well?

That might actually be interesting, in an academic sort of way. Perhaps he was a rake. She'd never met one of those. Of course, if he was a rake in Shropshire, he must be even more bored than she anticipated being. There was something rather sad about a man who was reduced to deflowering dairy maids and duelling with farm boys. As far as Felicity was concerned, all the quality sinning happened in London.

Or perhaps Italy.

And he had the nerve to call her a wayward girl. It was an improvement on the 'unrepentant hoyden' that her father had accused her of being, but not much. She supposed her father was right. She did not feel sorry for what she had done. She was the very definition of unrepentant.

If the Marquess of Woodley found her unsuitable, so be it. But he should explain why he wandered the countryside looking like an absent-minded vagrant. She might be ruined, but he was an eccentric who should not point his finger.

If they were not to be friends she did not need to be charming, simply polite.

As the first course arrived she ignored the man across from her and glanced up the table at Lady Ophelia, remarking, 'I have never been to Shropshire before. The countryside is very lovely.'

'We find it so,' her hostess agreed. 'But Martin knows it better than I do—he spends much of his time outdoors. He likes birds, you see.' Then she looked at her nephew, as if expecting him to carry the rest of the conversation.

The Marquess's fork froze halfway to his mouth, a bite of squab dangling in the air between them. Then he lowered it slowly and reached for his wine, taking a deep drink but offering no other answer.

'Do you shoot?' Felicity enquired, staring across the table at him.

'He draws pictures,' Lady Ophelia said, before he could speak for himself. 'You must show her your watercolours, Martin. They are really very good.'

This last was directed to Felicity with a proud smile.

'Next you will be asking me to play the pianoforte after dinner,' poor Martin replied, with an exasperated expression.

'Can you?' Felicity asked.

'Certainly not,' he snapped. 'And I do not *like* birds. I am writing a scholarly book on the local species, including colour plates of them in their natural habitats.'

'But you don't like birds?' she said, confused.

'I appreciate them,' he said, as if that should make some difference in the conversation. Then he smiled at her, eager to change the subject. 'I am glad you are enjoying Shropshire. What brings you here, Miss Morgan?'

Now it was her turn to be trapped in wordless confusion. She should have prepared an answer to the question, but she had not thought that anyone would be rude enough to ask it on the first day.

'Her grandmother is a friend of mine,' Ophelia answered for her, giving her nephew a firm look to close that avenue of conversation. 'Perhaps the next time you are in London, Martin, you might pay a call on her family in return.'

'Do you go to London often?' Felicity asked, turning to him.

'No.' This was delivered in a firm tone that declared that line of enquiry permanently closed as well.

'I have not been in years,' Ophelia supplied, turning the conversation again. 'You must tell me all about the recent fashions.'

Felicity did so, in excruciating detail, while the Marquess focused on his dinner. Then the talk turned to the food, which was proclaimed by all to be well prepared. And finally there was a brief overview of recent politics, upon which Felicity decided to have no opinion, fearing that any views she might venture would be declared wrongheaded by the Marquess, who seemed to be going out of his way to be disagreeable.

When the dessert course was finished Woodley made his excuses and left them for the evening. His aunt escorted him to the door and encouraged him to ride safely on the half-mile to his home.

She returned to Felicity in the parlour, shaking her head. 'It really is a shame about Martin.'

'What is?' Felicity asked, unable to contain her curiosity.

'He was not always the recluse you have met today. To look at him, you would not know that he was one of the most sought-after bachelors of the 1812 Season. He will be a duke when his father dies, but I doubt at the rate he is going that he will stir himself to go back to town even for Parliament.'

'A scandal?' she said, almost afraid to hear the details that had not been shared at dinner.

'Hardly,' Ophelia said, with another shake of her head. 'One night at Almack's he met Lady Emma Carstairs and never looked at another woman. They were married within the month, and the world had never seen a happier couple.'

'Married?' she repeated, surprised.

'For a year, at least,' Ophelia said. 'She was with child in a few months and they were both eagerly awaiting the birth. But the baby was breech and the delivery difficult.' Ophelia shook her head, sadly this time. 'There was nothing the surgeon could do to save them. He lost both wife and son. It has been three years now, and he shows no sign of recovering from their deaths. He divides his time between the house and the grounds, sketching birds and making notes for a book that I doubt he will ever finish. It is the solitude he craves, not the pursuit of knowledge.

I have tried to get him to return to society, but he claims to be too busy with his work.'

'That is very sad,' said Felicity dutifully.

And it was. She could imagine the man who had dined with them in better days, laughing and chatting, perhaps casting lingering looks at a woman down the table from him, sharing secret jokes with her. And at night, when they came together again, sharing gossip about the evening, his hand would be gentle on her shoulder as his head dipped to brush her ear with his lips.

The hair at the side of her neck stood up, as if in response to a whisper in her own ear, and she shuddered.

'Are you chilled?' Lady Ophelia asked, reaching for a shawl that was draped over the back of a chair and handing it to her.

Rather than explain, Felicity nodded and accepted the wrap.

'This old house can be rather draughty,' the older woman replied with a sympathetic smile. 'And, of course, there are the spirits…'

'I beg your pardon?' Felicity said, glancing around her at the shadows gathering in the corners of the room.

'The spirits,' Lady Ophelia repeated. 'This house is haunted, you see.'

Felicity blinked back at her for a moment, unsure of what to say. Then she managed, 'By whom?'

'I am not sure,' her hostess replied. 'But if you hear noises in the night it is better to remain in bed than to investigate them. The atmosphere in the upstairs corridor can be quite…disturbing.' She gave a shudder that had nothing to do with the temperature of the room. Then she reached for her needlework. 'It is still an hour before bed, my dear. Perhaps you might read to me. There is a book of sermons here that should be quite edifying.'

Spirits.

Felicity tried to hide her feelings of glee at this latest development. She had never been haunted before. Perhaps this trip would not be as boring as she had first feared.

But the promised ghosts showed no sign of appearing in the very ordinary sitting room she shared with her hostess, so Felicity took up the proffered book and they spent the rest of the evening in peace.

Chapter Three

Martin rode home in pensive silence, handing his reins to the groom who waited at his front door and stalking into the house and up the stairs. The evening had not precisely been a disaster. But it had been damned awkward, and he feared it was the first in a long string of such painful dinners now that Miss Morgan was in residence.

When he reached the first landing he stopped, as he always did, at the portrait of himself and Emma that took pride of place at the end of the little gallery. It was his habit to wish her goodnight before going to his room, and this night he had more to say than usual.

As always, she greeted him with a smile. He was not so lost to reality that he expected her painted visage to change. But sometimes it seemed to him that he could read the thoughts she would have had and hear her answers to him as he spoke. It was a small comfort in a world that had scant little of that left for him.

'There is a woman,' he said to her, with no preamble, shaking his head in disgust.

There was bound to be eventually.

The thought shocked him, for it was not one that he had intended to think, and nor did he want to imagine it on the lips of the woman who had been his one true love.

'Not a woman for me. Just a girl who is visiting Ophelia,' he corrected.

A beautiful girl.

'Not as beautiful as some,' he said, staring up at the painting with a pang of longing.

Different.

She was different. Truly lovely in her own way. He would be lying if he denied it.

'Next you will be telling me that a change is as good as a rest,' he muttered.

There had been little of either in the last three years. The days were all the same. The nights were all lonely. Even the food did not change. He had seen to that.

Today was different.

It had been. But had it been better? It was too soon to tell. But it was unfair of him to pretend that the presence of Miss Morgan had made it any worse.

She had done nothing objectionable to him and he had been nothing but odious to her—from forgetting her at the junction to baiting her throughout dinner. If there had been a problem with today, it had been him and his difficult nature.

He smiled up at the painting and shook his head in remorse. 'If you were here, you would scold me into a better humour. You left too soon.'

Till death us do part.

He stared up at the picture, annoyed to be reminded of the fact that he had lost her.

You don't have to be alone.

'I don't mind,' he said hurriedly, alarmed at the direction his thoughts were taking.

But are you happy?

He did not want to think on that, either.

'Content,' he murmured, trying to ignore the creeping feelings of restlessness that had plagued him today.

Liar.

He sighed. It was one thing to lie to Ophelia, and quite another to lie to himself. 'But what am I to do about it?'

To this there was no answer—at least none he was ready to make. So he touched his fingers lightly to his lips in a parting salute and went on up the stairs to bed.

* * *

At ten o'clock, Felicity bade her hostess a good night and proceeded to her room. There, she prepared for bed, then sat down to write the letter she had promised, on the single sheet of paper provided. As she'd feared, the writing desk in her room was empty of proper supplies, leaving her with only a single quill and an almost empty inkwell.

It was not enough.

Even if she went back downstairs and forced the lock on the desk in the sitting room she had seen only a small stack of paper in the drawer—hardly enough to suit her needs for more than a day or two. And to steal that would be to lose the trust of the woman who had been set to care for her and would probably result in more strictures. One sheet at a time would have to do.

She sat down, picked up the quill, and wrote a tedious account of her travels, turning the paper a quarter turn and writing the second page crosswise, to make the best use of what she had been given. It was a boring missive, with too much detail about the inns she had stayed at on the way, the quality of the beds and the food there, then a final assurance that she was safe with Lady Ophelia and a promise that she would cause no more trouble.

She did not bother to mention the Marquess, since

she was sure a true account of their acquaintance would only disappoint her mother. Perhaps once she knew the man better she would be able to describe him as pleasant company. But for now the best she could say was that he was handsome, but rude.

When she ran out of space to write she sanded the letter, folded and addressed it, and placed it on the edge of the table to give to the maid for the outgoing mail.

Duty done, she blew out the candle and climbed into bed, still wide awake, to await the wandering spirits that her hostess had promised her. She had never been in a purportedly haunted house before, and nor was she positive that she believed in such things. But she did appreciate a good ghost story, and hoped that the local haunting would not disappoint her.

For now, she listened eagerly, waiting for whatever might come.

The scratching of mice in the walls seemed louder than it did at home—as if the animals were not the wee things she was used to, but sizeable country rats. Outside the window there was the fluttering of a bat or some night bird that made the moonlit shadows dance across the floor in a most disturbing way. Then came the steady chiming of the long-case clock in the hall, faintly counting out eleven o'clock.

Perhaps it was her own imagination—which was prodigious—but she thought she heard footsteps in the corridor. She watched the place where the door met the floor, expecting to see the faint glow of light as a servant passed with a hand candle, but the space remained as velvety black as ever, though the steps continued past her room, fading away as they reached the stairs that led to the next floor.

She lay frozen for at least an hour, trying to imagine what eldritch horror might lie on the other side of the door. It was probably nothing more than a maid, running some final errand before bed, but Lady Ophelia's hints had raised her hopes for something that would lessen the boredom. The least this phantom could do—if such it was—was to wail pitifully and perhaps clank a chain or two.

But nothing occurred. She felt no unearthly presence, heard no mysterious wailings or dragging chains, and saw no spectral mist. There was not even an unexplained chill in the air. Truth be told, her new room was cheerful in daylight and warm and comfortable in the night. The bed was snug and tight, and the sheets smelled of lavender. It was all quite mundane.

The lack of proper haunting left her no choice but to entertain herself by making up stories in her head to pass the time before sleep. As she often did at home, she lay in the dark, imagining lurid fantasies of kidnap and rescue by handsome saviours.

Tonight, her heroine was an innocent girl who had been banished by her parents to a distant land, held captive in a prison with only an old woman for company. To increase the drama, she added a ghost, lurking at the cell doorway, pacing the stone halls of a castle with walls too steep to be scaled by anyone but the stalwart hero.

And if the rescuer had taken on a passing resemblance to the Marquess of Woodley she had no intention of admitting it—even to herself.

Chapter Four

The next day, as he guided his gig down the rutted lane towards Vicar's Hill, Martin squinted into the cheerful sunshine, hating the morning and everything in it. Today even the sound of the birds singing in the trees—something that normally gave him great pleasure—was grating on his nerves.

He was not sure why. He had not drunk to excess the previous evening, nor had he overindulged in the food served at dinner. He was not bilious or blue-devilled. He simply felt as if he was. His head ached as if he'd tried to outdrink a sailor.

It was probably that he had not slept well. His dreams had been haunted by large brown eyes and a faintly sarcastic smile—and the sound of his aunt announcing that he liked to draw pictures of birds. She'd made him sound like a child, scribbling on the walls.

It was not as if he'd wanted to impress Miss Morgan. Last night he had promised himself to treat her politely—nothing more than that. It was simply that her presence had made him aware of how much he had changed in the last few years. And not for the better.

Before he had married he'd loved London and the people in it. The balls, the routs, the intellectual stimulation of his club—everything about the place had been fodder for his soul. But now even sitting down to read the news of the day seemed overwhelming. Last night's dinner conversation had left him exhausted and out of sorts.

He had blamed Miss Morgan for the change in his mood, but perhaps it was he who was the problem and she the much-needed solution. A bit of small talk with a stranger would do him good. But she was a cure to be taken in moderation, lest people think he meant to court her. He certainly did not intend anything so extreme.

Perhaps, after checking on his orders at the shop in the village, he would indulge in a glass of ale to numb the pain in his head and take the edge off his embarrassment. That, and time, would be enough of a cure to start with. He suspected that now that he'd gone to the obligatory dinner at the dower house he need not see the girl again for at least a week.

But he was not to be that lucky.

As he turned on to the main road she was there in front of him, walking towards Vicar's Hill in a determined fashion, bonnet tied tight and reticule swinging at her side. As she had been last night, she was wearing what he assumed was the latest London fashion, a ruffled gown with a blue wool pelisse, and dainty boots that had been designed for paved streets and carriage rides, not two-mile hikes through the country.

He sighed. The coward he had become was tempted to drive by without comment. But it would be most ungentlemanly of him to pull around her and leave her in the mud. And he owed her a ride, since he'd neglected to give her one yesterday.

She glanced back over her shoulder at the sound of his horse, then turned to face front again, moving to the side of the road, ready to let him pass. She was all but giving him permission to leave her.

He wavered for a moment longer, then pulled alongside her and stopped. 'Good morning, Miss Morgan.'

'Good morning, Lord Woodley,' she said, with a dip of her head, then took another step.

'I assume you are going to the village, as am I. May I offer you a ride?'

She glanced at him, and at the single seat in his small carriage. 'You must pardon me for asking, sir, but is it not rather improper for me to ride with you without a maid or some sort of chaperon?'

If she had been sent to rusticate, her worries about her reputation were too little and too late. But he bit back the rebuke and replied, 'Etiquette is somewhat more relaxed in the country. The people of the village all know me and can vouch for my character. In fact, they would think far less of me if I were to abandon you to carry on making your journey on foot.'

She hesitated for a moment, shifting from foot to foot in a way that made him suspect she was already regretting her choice of shoes.

Then she said, 'Very well,' and stepped forward to accept the hand he offered to help her onto the seat beside him.

He shook the reins and they were off again, riding in silence towards the village.

'Thank you,' she said suddenly. 'For the ride, I mean. I did not want to trouble your aunt to see if she had a vehicle I might use. She was asleep, you see.'

'So late in the day?'

'She had already risen. But she suggested that I read to her after luncheon,' Miss Morgan said with a sigh. 'It was a book of sermons…'

'How edifying,' he said, and could not help a small shudder of sympathy.

'Indeed,' she said. 'They made me quite drowsy as well. I thought perhaps a walk…' Her words trailed away and she stared in front of her again.

This came as a surprise. In his experience Ophelia was not prone to naps or sermonising. Perhaps she had changed her reading habits to set a good example to Miss Morgan, only to be bored to unconsciousness by it. No wonder the poor girl had escaped the house.

Which brought him to his own treatment of her and the nagging guilt he felt at it. 'About last night…' he began. 'As you were coming into the room I said something most unkind.'

She waved a hand in dismissal, as if she suspected the apology he was going to make. 'I think your aunt fancies herself a matchmaker. While it is very kind of her, I assure you I am not seeking marriage.'

Not seeking marriage? This was a surprise. Or perhaps it was just her way of saying that she was not interested in him—which was exactly what he had hoped to hear. And yet also rather insulting.

'At the moment, you mean?' he said with a nod.

'At all,' she said giving him a firm smile.

'You are a decided spinster?' he asked, surprised. Whoever had taken her honour must have put her off men.

'I prefer to think of myself as happily unmarried,'

she said, smiling into the distance, as if she could see something he could not. 'But if you must call me that, then I suppose I am a spinster.'

'Perhaps you have not met the right man,' he said, and then regretted it. The tone he'd used sounded rather as if he was volunteering for the position.

'Perhaps I have met enough men to confirm my suspicions about them,' she said, still not looking at him.

Whatever her experience, it had been the deciding factor, he was sure.

'Marriage is not such a bad thing, really,' he said, thinking back on his own.

She must have noticed the wistfulness in his voice, for she turned to him now with a look of sympathy. 'Your aunt told me of your loss. I am sorry.'

'You needn't be,' he said, releasing a sigh. 'While I was married, I was very happy. Too happy, perhaps. Such joy was not meant to last.'

'And you do not intend to risk your heart again,' she said with a sage nod. 'I do not blame you for it. Marriage is not for everyone.'

He nodded back, relieved. It appeared that his aunt's plans were all for naught. If the two of them agreed on nothing else, it was the complete unsuitability of any match between them.

If that was true, then he had nothing to fear. He

was raising no false hopes in her with this association. And as long as he was paying polite attention to her his aunt would stop bothering him about his unsociable behaviour. The visit from this attractive stranger could be an unexpected boon after all.

He smiled to himself and gave the reins a shake to pick up their pace.

Felicity stared at the road ahead of them, and at the village growing closer with each step the horse took. Lord Woodley's story was a sad one, and if it had made him a bit of a curmudgeon she supposed he had every reason to be bitter.

It was also quite romantic. Some girls might have sighed over such a tale and got ideas.

She was not some girl.

It did give her ideas, of course. Just not about him. At least, not about the two of them.

She considered his past from all sides, and could easily imagine Lady Woodley, her hopes and dreams cut short, and her husband, bending over the childbed, broken by the loss.

It was the stuff of great tragedy, but there was great hope in the unwritten sequel. If he could overcome his grief he would be the man he had been, but stronger. Perhaps there was a way she could help him—if only by offering her friendship.

'Vicar's Hill,' he announced, breaking her reverie.

She looked around her, trying not to seem as disappointed as she felt at the sight of the place, which was not much more than a cluster of cottages around a village green.

'Was there something in particular you were looking for?' he asked, smiling at her discomfiture.

'A stationer's?' she said hopefully.

At this, he laughed. 'I will take you to the shop. Perhaps they will have what you need. But probably not.'

He parked the carriage along the side of the high street and helped her down from the seat, gesturing to the door of the nearest building.

Inside was an amazing conglomeration of items so varied that she was not sure where to look. There were a few books on one side of the door, all several years old, with a placard listing a price for their rental. On the other she found a mismatched set of china and a collection of pans and kettles.

She moved through the room, stopping to admire the ladies' clothing section, anchored by a small selection of muslins and an equally limited number of trims. On the table in front of them was a stack of fashion plate magazines which were seasons out of date. If this was all that was available, she suspected that the young ladies in the area had no choice but to dress all alike. But next to them she found a set of walking boots that appeared to be her size, and she searched her reticule for the coins necessary to purchase them.

The Marquess was on the other side of the room, just past the men's clothing, enquiring after an order of millet to feed his birds. When she was sure he was paying her no mind, she worked her way over to the stationery shelf and laid her hand on the little pile of paper for sale there.

It was a penny a sheet, and even if she bought it all it would not be enough for her purpose. She could order more from London, she supposed. But Lady Ophelia was likely to find out and take it away from her. And, of course, there was the matter of money. Her father had confiscated her savings before putting her on the mail coach, leaving her barely enough in her purse to avoid embarrassment during the visit. She would run through it in a month if she had to keep buying paper.

'Did you find what you were looking for?' The Marquess glanced across the shop at her.

She held up the boots in answer, hoping he had forgotten her earlier question about a stationer's.

He nodded. 'Very sensible. You will need them. There is much walking to be done in the country.'

'I have noticed,' she said, thinking of the way he had abandoned her yesterday.

He gave her an apologetic smile. 'When I am working I sometimes lose track of time. But now that you are here I mean to make up for my earlier lapse. If you need anything, all you have to do is ask it of me.'

She thought of the paper, and wondered if Lady Ophelia had warned him against giving her any. Then she said, 'Thank you. I will do that.'

Sometime soon, when they were not in such a public place, she must find out what he knew of the restrictions that had been set upon her.

With their purchases made, they left the shop and stood looking up and down the high street, which was very short.

'Was there anything else you wished to do while here?' the Marquess asked.

'*Is* there anything else to do?' she asked, equally curious.

'I could take you to see the vicar,' he mused. 'Although I doubt a visit today will be very interesting for you. He has no wife or sister to hostess for him—only a housekeeper.'

'Perhaps I shall wait until Sunday and attend the service with Ophelia,' she said, wondering how much that man had heard of her scandal.

'Or perhaps I could invite you and the vicar to the great house for dinner and cards,' he offered.

'It has been a long time since we have had a fourth for whist.'

'I should like that,' she replied.

It would certainly be an improvement on reading sermons and dozing in the sitting room.

Lord Woodley stared down the street, searching for anything else that might interest her. 'There is the inn... It has a public room within, where it is possible to have a mug of ale and a sandwich.'

'I have already eaten,' she said.

'Then, unless you need to purchase groceries or shoe a horse, you have seen all of Vicar's Hill,' he said with a shrug.

She had known that it was a small village. But she had not considered what that meant until seeing it in person. What was she going to do with her days? Especially if she could not find something to write upon?

She did her best to hide her dismay and turned to face the Marquess. 'I suppose I will go back to Lady Ophelia's, then. When you are ready, of course.'

'At your service,' he said, helping her up into the carriage and heading back up the road towards the dower house.

They travelled in silence, while she considered and rejected various topics of conversation, at last settling on one that had confused her the night before.

'You have lived in the area for many years, have you not?'

He nodded. 'And visited often in my youth, as well. The estate has always belonged to my family.'

'Have you ever heard the story of the dower house ghost?'

The Marquess started and turned to her, confused. 'What story? What ghost?'

'Your aunt told me of it last night. I was wondering if there might be a legend that she had not heard, for she claimed that the house was haunted but said nothing of the cause.'

'On the contrary. I have never heard the story at all.' He frowned. 'She has not told me of any problems, and nor has she mentioned being frightened in her own home.'

'She did not seem bothered by it,' Felicity said hurriedly. 'She was very matter-of-fact about the whole thing. But it made me wonder if there was a family history.'

Living with a spectral weeping widow or a grey lady stalking the halls would be quite interesting, if the only highlight of her week was to be a hand of whist with the vicar.

Her companion was still frowning—probably worrying about his aunt. 'There is none, as far as I know. But if you wish you may look in the library at the main house to see if there is anything in the journals or letters about a haunting. Make free with the rest of the books as well. The selection in the shop is very poor, and reading will help you pass the time.'

'Thank you,' she said, relieved. 'Reading anything other than sermons would be a welcome change.'

He laughed, giving the reins a shake to urge the horses around a curve in the road. As he did so his sleeve brushed her arm, making her aware of how close they sat and how alone they were.

In all her time in London she had never gone riding with a gentleman, not wanting to encourage the suits of men she had no intention of accepting. But now that they had agreed there was no future in it, sitting here beside Lord Woodley was surprisingly pleasant.

'If not sermons, what do you enjoy reading?' he asked.

'Novels,' she said automatically.

He responded with a scoffing noise and another shake of the reins.

'You do not approve?' she asked, casting a sidelong look at his handsome profile.

'They are all right for some, I suppose,' he replied.

'They are very popular in London,' she replied.

'I am not surprised,' he said with a dismissive

laugh, as if he expected nothing less than reading novels from the sort of gadabouts who lived in the city.

'And what do *you* prefer?' she asked, resigned.

'Histories. Poetry, on occasion. Scholarly works...'

'Edifying prose,' she said with a sigh.

'But not sermons,' he took a sidelong look at her. 'Perhaps you will not enjoy my library after all.'

'I am sure there is something in it that I will enjoy,' she said.

If the writing desk there was unlocked, a visit would be more satisfying than he could possibly imagine.

Chapter Five

Martin delivered Miss Morgan to the dower house, letting himself in to visit his aunt as she went upstairs to change out of her walking dress.

Ophelia beamed at him, probably more encouraged than she should have been at the sight of them arriving together. 'I see you found my guest,' she said.

'And got her safely to the village and back,' he finished for her. 'It did not take very long to show her that there is nothing to be done there.'

Ophelia frowned at him. 'Do not underrate the charms of village life. I am sure, given time, Felicity will come to enjoy it as much as we do. And the May Festival is almost here. That is always an eventful day.'

He answered with a hollow laugh. 'She is used to living in London, with its constant entertainments.'

If her parents had chosen this as her place of punishment, they must have had a reason. It must be a special kind of hell for her to be here, where there was nothing to do but take vigorous walks and wait for someone to put up the maypole.

'She is not who you think she is,' Ophelia said, noting his frown. 'You must give the girl a chance.'

'To do what?' he replied.

'To win your approval, at least,' she said. 'At this juncture in her life she needs all the friends she can find.'

If she was a fallen woman, that was probably true.

'I am resolved to treat her better than I did yesterday—which should not be difficult. My behaviour at dinner was sorely lacking in hospitality.' Then he remembered the conversation he'd had with her in the carriage and pointed an accusing finger at his aunt. 'But what sort of friend makes up fustian about ghosts in the dower house?'

'Oh, that,' Ophelia said with a laugh. 'Felicity is an impressionable girl, with a very active imagination. I see no harm in giving her a reason to keep to her room at night, rather than setting a curfew.'

'I have given her permission to research the matter in my library,' he said, with a disgusted shake of his head.

'All the better. It will give her a harmless activity to fill her empty days.'

'Fruitless as well,' he said, surprised at his aunt's deceitful nature.

Ophelia shrugged. 'Perhaps. Or perhaps she will

find something in the library that interests her as much as your birds do you.'

He shrugged. Researching someone else's family was a harmless enough pastime, even if it wasn't as useful as the pursuit he'd selected to ease his own boredom.

But why had he chosen his particular hobby? He had shown no interest in birds when Emma was alive. Then he vaguely remembered a conversation with Ophelia when she had bemoaned the lack of scholarly interest in the local fauna...

'Was that your plan for me, as well?' he asked, giving her a probing look. 'Did you hint me into birdwatching just to see me busy?'

'You needed an occupation,' she replied. 'You were at loose ends, with no reason to move forward. I simply nudged you in a direction you would have found yourself, in time.'

'Or perhaps not,' he said, still not sure if he should be grateful for her interference. 'In the future, please limit your meddling to Miss Morgan's future and leave my life alone.'

'Of course,' his aunt replied, with a smile that was too sweet to be believed.

Shaking his head, Martin let himself out.

When Felicity returned to the main floor, after changing, the Marquess had taken his leave and

Lady Ophelia was alone in the sitting room, darning stockings.

She set them aside and looked up with a smile. 'Did you enjoy your trip to the village, my dear?'

'It was most...' She stopped, for the only honest way to finish that sentence was with the word *disappointing*. 'The Marquess was most kind to give me a ride,' she said, for gratitude was a better path to take.

'He told me he has offered you the use of his library as well,' she said, still smiling.

'I thought it might be interesting to learn about the house and the family,' she said. It was a half-truth, at best. It was not as if she would not look into those things after she had got her hands on some paper.

'That is an excellent idea,' Lady Ophelia said. 'It is good that you should find a way to pass the time, and you will find the library at the great house is much better than the poor room I have here.'

'This is not so bad,' she said hurriedly.

'But it does not give you the chance to visit a gentleman who is both titled and handsome,' Ophelia announced.

'That is not what I was thinking at all,' she said hurriedly.

Ophelia responded with a small, frustrated shake of her head. 'If not, then perhaps you should be. I am well aware that this visit was intended as a punishment by your parents, Felicity, and I doubt they mean to relent in their discipline of you until you are properly married and out of their control.'

'But what if I do not wish to marry?' she responded. 'I am quite capable of taking care of myself, both physically and financially.'

'If they allow you to do so,' Ophelia finished for her. 'You understand that girls have been committed to institutions for displaying the sort of independent thinking you seem prone to?'

'I am not mad for wishing to remain single,' Felicity insisted. 'Nor for anything else I have done thus far.'

'I am aware of that,' Ophelia said, with a sympathetic smile. 'But your father seems to have a different opinion on the matter. And if you do not come round to his way of thinking and find yourself a husband, there is no telling what he might resort to—just to keep you in line.'

'And you agreed to help him,' Felicity said, unable to keep the tone of accusation from her voice.

'Only because I thought it would be easier for you to be here than in some of the other places he might have chosen,' Lady Ophelia replied. 'I gave my word not to indulge your hobbies by supplying the materials for them, and I do not wish to break it. But I am also an old lady prone to frequent naps and not very observant.' She winked. 'I cannot be expected to watch you every minute, and I shall have no idea what you might get up to while my back is turned.'

'Thank you for your understanding,' Felicity said, relieved that she would not be forced to deceive the old woman, who obviously planned to look the other way. 'But that does not mean that I intend to pursue your nephew, who is no more interested in marrying than I am.'

'Then choose someone else,' Ophelia said. 'Despite what you think, you will have more freedom as a married woman than you do now—and even more than that should you become a widow.'

Felicity laughed. 'I cannot marry with the hope that my husband dies before me.'

Ophelia shrugged in response. 'I am just saying that if you are patient there might be more than one way to achieve the ends you are looking for. Now, let us prepare for dinner. We will have a quiet evening. Just the two of us. And I promise to say no more about it.'

Chapter Six

Felicity awoke the next morning, fresh and untroubled, and thoroughly disappointed by the lack of mysterious screams in the night. A ghost would have been far less worrying than her hostess's suggestion that she become a bride in the hope of being widowed.

That thought had occupied her as she'd lain awake, waiting for her ghost. Would she be expected to hurry the death of this imaginary man to achieve her goals? How would she go about it? Poison, probably. Not that she knew where to get such a thing. From a doctor, perhaps? A handsome young one, sympathetic to her misery, but unable to help her in any other way...

And the husband would have to be truly evil before she would consider murder. Which left her imagining a miserable marriage and an equally miserable life while awaiting escape. Was that really what Ophelia hoped for for her? And what did it say of that woman's wedded life that she was so much happier now?

Her nephew was a far better argument for marriage than she was. For a brief time he had been truly happy. His wife had been as well. At the thought of them, she felt a lump rise in her throat. She did not think it was the beginning of sympathetic tears, though the story made her ache with sadness. Rather, it felt as if there was something she needed to say, but she could not find the words.

How curious. Normally her imagination had no trouble in coming up with entire conversations. But when she thought of the Marquess her mind was a jumble.

Probably because, unlike the men she made up in her head, his behaviour in real life so often surprised her. She had not expected he would apologise for calling her wayward, and it had been unexpectedly pleasant riding with him yesterday. When she had come to the country she'd had no idea that she might find a gentleman so kind.

It was probably because they could set courtship aside and be their true selves. Life would be much easier if all relationships were so clearly defined.

After a light breakfast, she informed Ophelia of

her plans to spend the day at the great house, reading in the library.

'So early in the day?' her hostess asked, surprised.

'The Marquess's offer to use his home is most generous, and I mean to make use of it whenever possible,' she replied. 'I am eager to see what I can find out about the history of the house.'

'But he will be out in the woods with his birds,' Ophelia said, with a moue of disappointment.

'It would not be proper for me to call on him when he was at home,' Felicity reminded her.

'Nonsense,' the old lady said with a scoff. 'The place is full of servants who are as good as any chaperon. I am sure your parents would not mind you going there. I certainly do not.'

It was clear that she had not given up her hopes that the two of them might take an interest in each other.

He did interest her, of course. Just not in the sort of way that would lead to marriage. But there was no reason to disappoint her, so Felicity smiled and said, 'Well, I am sure I cannot get into too much trouble, as long as you know where I am.'

A short time later she set off down the road and soon turned up the drive to the Woodley mansion.

It was the first time Felicity had been invited to the home of a titled gentleman, and she supposed she should be excited by it. Of course, after seeing the Marquess in his birding clothes it was hard to take his rank seriously. He did not behave with the dignity she expected from the son of a duke. Although she could hardly be one to judge eccentricity. By her parents' standards she was quite odd herself.

Well, if they were both outcasts, then maybe he would understand the needs and desires that had landed her in this place and be sympathetic to her goals, should she explain them.

She was walking up the drive to the house now, and was rather disappointed to find it looked to be made of the same clean white stone as the dower house. There was to be no gothic ruin in her future—which was just as well, she supposed. Ruins were likely damp and uncomfortable, and difficult to work in. When she read and wrote she preferred a warm fire and a decent amount of light.

If that was what she wanted, the inside of the house was exactly to her taste.

When she'd lived in London, she had read in Ackermann's Repository about the latest styles of furniture and design and had assumed that all peers spent most of their time redecorating, to keep up with the fashion of the day. But this house was almost shabby in its decoration. If Woodley's late wife had done anything upon moving in Felicity could not see it, for the walls and the furniture seemed to be a good twenty years out of date.

That said, everything was clean and sturdy, and there was a sort of homely feel to the place—as if each piece had been chosen for maximum functionality. The tables in the library were large and solid, the chairs deep and comfortable, and a good light for reading shone in through the windows, which were tall and wide and looked out on a pleasant garden.

According to the servants, the lord of the manor was already in the woods, as she had expected he would be. Apparently he was gone most days from mid-morning until the sun was almost setting. Despite what Lady Ophelia had hoped for, there was little chance that her presence in his house would be noted, or that they would even meet. She would be able to work here in peace for as long as she wanted, interrupted only by the housekeeper, who arrived a short time later and offered her refreshments, before directing her to the set of shelves devoted to the family's history.

Felicity thanked the woman and took down a volume to enjoy with her tea. It was dry reading, involving the crops planted by local tenants and the amount of rents totalled for each month. There were no personal details of the family members at all, and certainly no stories of mysterious deaths or unexplained happenings in either this house or its dower house up the road.

But she had not really expected a direct explanation—at least not in the very first book she chose. Since she had an ulterior motive in coming here, she was far more interested in setting up a regular schedule and having the servants accept her presence there as a normal part of the day.

Once she had reached the point where she could stand no more tedious details of household accounting, she wandered over to the writing desk that had been her goal all along and tested the drawers.

Unlike those at Lady Ophelia's house, they were unlocked. But unfortunately they contained nothing. The inkwell was empty and the only quill in the stand was old and cracked. It was disappointing, for she had hoped to begin her work here, under the guise of taking notes on the family history. But it seemed that this library was used exclusively for reading.

That did not mean there weren't other rooms nearby that had paper...

There was a door beside the desk that led to an adjoining room and she tried the handle. It opened easily, and brought her into what appeared to be the master's study.

She hesitated on the doorstep—but for only a moment, before convincing herself that if Lord Wood-ley had wanted the room to be private he would have locked it. And if he used it for his work, it would be properly supplied with writing materials—drawing materials as well.

And there, on a table by the window, was a sketch-pad and a stack of rich, cotton pulp paper, perfect for watercolour painting. The top sheet was a finished study of a pair of grosbeaks—one in flight, showing a flash of red underwing, the other seated on a nest.

She admired it for a moment, trailing a finger along the edge to rest near the word *Woodley* in neat script at the bottom. The Marquess had a real talent for his work, and his enthusiasm for the subject was expressed in the fluid lines and lifelike painting. If this was a good example of his work, she hoped to persuade him to show her more.

Then she set it aside and returned to searching, trying the drawers of the massive desk that occupied a prominent place in the room. The centre drawer was locked, but the right hand one gave easily, to reveal a stack of creamy writing paper just waiting for her to fill with words. And she swore she could smell the ink in the well...wet and dark, ready to use.

She closed her eyes and inhaled deeply, drinking in the scent. Then she ran her fingertips over the top sheet of paper in the stack. Perhaps her parents were right and there was something wrong with her, for without pen and paper she felt like an addict who had been denied her opium. In the last seven days she had written nothing but that single boring letter. But now—finally—she could begin again.

She grabbed a handful of sheets from the desk drawer, crumpling the edges in her eagerness to get them away, and was so transfixed by the excitement of her find that she did not hear approaching footsteps until they were almost upon her.

'What are you doing in my study?'

The Marquess stood in the doorway, his large frame blocking the light that streamed in on her from the library.

'Nothing,' she said automatically, hiding the paper she was holding behind her back. It was a foolish gesture, for he was across the room in two steps to grip her wrists and pull them to her front again, so he could expose the theft.

But it was clear that he could not understand what it was he was seeing, even after it was revealed to him. He stared from the paper to her in confusion.

'The desk in the library was empty,' she said, feeling her cheeks flush in embarrassment.

'Why did you not simply ask the servants to bring you some paper?' he asked, staring at the blank sheets in her hand.

'Because I feared the answer would be no,' she said, staring at back at him and wondering if he had been warned about her. 'My father has seen to that, has he not?'

'Your father?' He gave her another blank look.

Could it be that her father's instructions for her punishment had not been shared with the Marquess? She'd assumed his aunt had told him all, but apparently not.

'In Lady Ophelia's house I am permitted one sheet of paper a day, so that I may write home to my mother,' she explained, and then blurted, 'But it is not enough.'

'That is the oddest thing I have ever heard,' he said, pulling the stack of paper from her hands and smoothing the pages she'd crushed.

'It is,' she agreed. 'And most unfair to me.' She held her hands out in supplication. 'If you could spare some paper… A ream, perhaps. Or two.' She gave him a hopeful smile.

Now he was staring at her as though she were a madwoman. That had been far too much to ask for. He must think her afflicted with some sort of mania pertaining to the hoarding of stationery.

'If that sounds excessive, I quite understand,' she said quickly, backing away from him. 'Even a few sheets would do.'

But it wouldn't. The work her father had burned had been nearly two hundred pages long and nowhere near complete. She hungered to rewrite— burned with the desire for it. It was her only hope for the future.

She wet her lips and took a step towards him, her resolve returned. 'No. That is not true. I must have at least a ream. I will do anything you wish, if only you will provide me with paper and keep my secret.'

'Anything?' he said, his tone and his expression blank.

As was often the case, she was being overly dramatic. Heroines in novels were often forced into the declaration she had just volunteered. They only said such things when begging for mercy from the villain of the piece. And what followed was usually a timely rescue by the hero, or some sort of nameless ruin that occurred off the page and left the poor girl lamenting for the rest of the book.

But life was not a gothic novel. The Marquess was a gentleman, and no threat to her honour. Even if she needed a rescuer, that man would probably not be bringing the paper she required. And as for ruin...

She was ruined already in the eyes of her family, and if the truth of her past escaped to the rest of the *ton* she would be too compromised to take up even a position as a governess or lady's companion. That left only one honest method to make her living in the world, and she could not do it without paper.

She gave the Marquess a direct look in response to his stare and said, 'Anything.'

To prove it, she closed her eyes, puckered her lips, and lunged over the desk to kiss him.

Their lips were together for only a moment, and it did not feel the least bit ruinous. In fact, it was quite pleasant. She had never kissed anyone before, but now that it had happened she wondered why. If she was losing her innocence with this behaviour it must be the sort of thing that trickled away slowly, for she did not think she was missing anything.

But just as she was trying to decide what to do next, he withdrew. He was staring at her, confused, as if considering his next step as well. He was probably going to be cross with her—as he had been when she'd screamed on the road. And a scolding was what she deserved, for she was not behaving as a polite young lady should. Her mother would be appalled when she learned of this, and she would be sent even farther away.

Scotland, perhaps. The Hebrides.

Then the Marquess peeled a single sheet from the stack of paper that he had been holding and handed it to her.

'That is not much paper,' she said, eyeing it suspiciously.

'That was not much of a kiss,' he replied with a wry smile.

His criticism was hardly fair. Since she had no experience in kissing, he should not expect her to know how best to do it. He was clearly disappointed by her technique, but she had thought it felt quite nice.

But maybe being nice wasn't the point. Passion was often compared to a raging fire, and she was sure she'd felt nothing like that. A spark, perhaps, but it had not had time to kindle. If she wanted to do this right she needed the right combination of skill and improvisation. More experimentation was required if she was to master this new skill.

Before she could think on it, and come to her senses, she lunged at him again, throwing her arms about him and planting her lips against his.

His mouth opened in shock, and without meaning to she thrust her tongue into it, then withdrew it just as quickly. But not before she got a taste of him. She had never known another person so intimately, and it made her tremble to the tips of her toes.

He pulled back, clearly even more surprised than she was, and stared at her, his breathing ragged and his fists balled at his sides, crushing the paper he had taken from her. For a moment she thought he was about to strike her, for he seemed to vibrate with violent emotion. Then he grabbed her and pulled her forward, until his lips were on hers again. This time he guided the kiss, and the awkwardness of the encounter disappeared.

His lips were soft and his movements slow, brushing back and forth on her mouth, easing her lips apart with a gentle nuzzle and running his tongue along the edge of her teeth as if daring her to bite him.

She responded with what felt like slack-jawed amazement. If this was what the books spoke of, in describing what happened when couples were alone together, they should find a better way. For she would never have imagined that behaviour as odd as this could be so wonderful. She felt warm all over, and tempted to loosen her stays… She was distinctly light-headed.

He must have sensed it, for the paper he had been holding dropped from his hand, sheets drifting to the floor as he stepped around the desk and pulled her body against his, splaying his hands against her shoulder blades and smoothing them down to her waist.

He was wearing his birding clothes, and she could feel the soft linen of his shirt under the open poacher's coat. She reached out to touch his bare throat, to feel the stubble on his jaw, to run her fingers through the hair at the back of his neck. She wanted to remember everything about this moment—the taste, the feelings, the fresh, woodsy smell of him and the warmth of his body seeping into hers.

He must be feeling the same, for his hands were moving gently over her, as if memorising her curves, pressing against her until she could feel the warmth of them through the thin muslin of her gown. His fingers found the fastenings at the back of her bodice, toying with them for a moment. Then they dropped to his sides and he stepped away from her.

Without him she felt weak, breathless, as though she needed another kiss just to keep life within her body. She gripped the edge of the desk with both hands, to keep from reaching out to beg for his return, and stared up into his face, trying to find the reason for his sudden rejection.

His eyes were dark, bottomless, and she thought she could gaze into them for ever, if only he would allow it. But his returning stare was guarded, as if a shutter had dropped to conceal his true feelings. His expression, which had been a confusing mix of emotions when he'd released her, became blank again.

'You will have all the paper you wish,' he said, in an emotionless voice. 'I will see to it that the library writing table is well stocked with pens and ink as well. If you wish to send letters from this address, simply leave them on the hall table with the rest of the outgoing post.'

'And what of Lady Ophelia, who would forbid me this?' she asked.

'I will say nothing of it to her. Nothing of any of this,' he added with an abrupt gesture of his hand.

'Nor will I,' she assured him.

'Very good.' Then he backed out of the room, leaving her alone again.

When he was clear of the study, Martin turned and hurried up the stairs towards his room, stopping at the portrait of Emma on the way.

'She kissed me,' he said, touching his temple as if to make sure that his head was still attached to his body. He had found her searching his desk. And then there had been some nonsense about doing anything for paper. And then… Chaos.

As usual, the painted Emma smiled back at him, blue eyes caught for ever in paint, alight with mirth. Today she looked as if she found his discomposure thoroughly amusing.

She kissed you? Not your fault, then, came the answering voice in his head.

'Twice,' he admitted.

Careless of you, his conscience replied.

'And then I kissed her back,' he said with a sigh of defeat.

What had possessed him to do such a thing?

It had been one thing to allow her the first kiss. It was clear that, whatever else her problems might be, Miss Morgan was a little bit impulsive. What with screaming on the road, hoarding paper and waylaying him in the study, she was given to fits of emotion and erratic behaviour. He must be on his guard when she was around or who knew what might happen?

He knew something almost had. When faced with the slightest feminine temptation he had found his plan to remain aloof and alone had crumpled like the paper she was seeking. He was a grown man, not some randy schoolboy. He should have better control of himself than to succumb to the charms of the first woman to cross his threshold.

It was probably the result of prolonged abstinence preying on his mind. A year or two ago he would have had the sense to disentangle himself from her arms after the first buss on the lips and give her the stern warning she deserved.

But he had stayed, unable to resist turning her awkward attempt into the first real kiss he'd had since losing Emma.

Did you enjoy it?

The question popped into his head, so alien and

surprising that it might as well have been the painting asking, come to life.

'Yes,' he said in a soft voice. 'Yes, I did. And if I had not been careful things would have got out of hand, right there on the desktop.'

In three years alone he had forgotten what it was like to hold a woman in his arms, to kiss and be kissed.

'It meant nothing,' he said, to remind himself of the fact. 'It was an accident and not some attempt to woo her.'

Suddenly he heard footsteps scurrying behind him and turned to find a maid, as embarrassed to find him talking to a picture as he was to be found. She was already running back down the hall towards the servants' stairs at the other end, probably going down to tell Mrs Spang that the master was babbling to himself in the portrait gallery.

Again.

Apparently he was as foolish as the girl in his study, if he got his only solace from talking to inanimate objects. Perhaps he was going mad.

But if it had not been for Miss Morgan... Soft, pliable, willing to do anything for a ream of paper...

In a way, it was rather insulting. The least she could have done was pretend that she could not resist his masculine charm. He glanced down at his sleeve and saw the same grubby coat he'd been wearing the first time they'd met. He was unshaven as well. The only saving grace was that he'd left his battered straw hat in the front hall.

Bumpkin.

She had obviously not wanted him at all. How could she, seeing him looking as he did?

He gave the portrait one last frustrated look, then stomped up the stairs and down the corridor to his room, slamming the door behind him. That display of temper was just as embarrassing as the rest of his behaviour, for it was loud enough to be heard by Miss Morgan, if she was still in the house.

He should not even be here with her, much less stomping around and embarrassing himself. But the day had been cloudy, his subjects uncooperative and, if he was honest, he had wondered if she would come to use the library on her pointless quest and had wanted to check on her. He had a good mind to tell her that there were no ghosts to investigate and to send her packing back to London. After what had happened, it would be the sensible thing to do.

But would it be fair to her? With her desperate gambit to get paper, he suspected she was eager to write to the man she had been sent here to be separated from. If her parents' strictures were keeping her from the man she loved, then it was heaping punishment on punishment to send her home, where the parting could be better enforced.

After the happiness he had experienced in his own marriage, he should appreciate her desire to find the same sort of love. If he let her use the library as promised, and she took advantage of his largesse to write to her lover, the fellow would know where to find her. Then they could reunite and plan a future without her parents' interference. Though she had sworn that she didn't want to marry, he suspected she would change her views immediately if the right man offered it to her.

Of course, this interpretation of her request for paper did not explain or justify the fact that she had kissed him to get it. That was not the sort of behaviour one expected of a woman in love with someone else. But Miss Morgan was a rather odd girl, and who could fathom the contents of such a mind as hers?

He feared her strangeness might be contagious, for he felt rather odd himself. It did not really matter if she went back to her lover, or to London, or perdition. But she must go somewhere—if only to keep him from kissing her again. Because the brief taste he'd had of those full red lips had not been enough. He wanted more of her.

She had to go, and take temptation with her. And when she was gone his life could go back to the way it had been: peaceful, quiet and safe.

Chapter Seven

After the Marquess left her, Felicity slunk back to the library, picked up one of the family histories and pretended to look for the dower house ghost. But it was impossible to concentrate on anything but the incident that had taken place in the study.

She had kissed him.

It had seemed like a good idea at the time. Like a punctuation mark at the end of a sentence, she had wanted to express how much she needed his help, and to say it in a way that could not be ignored.

Of course, she could have just said please…

But then he would not have kissed her back. At the memory, she could not keep from smiling, for it had been the most magical moment of her life. All the more exciting because, like in a really good story, she had no idea what would happen next.

Would they kiss again? And if they did would things progress from where they had ended today?

And progress towards what? She knew very little of the act of love beyond what she had read, and authors were vague on the details.

For example, no book she had read so far had captured the thrill she'd felt when their tongues met, or the excitement as he'd pulled her close.

Why had he even come back to the house? She had not expected discovery when she'd sneaked into the study. He was supposed to be away during the day. Had he come looking for her? Had he wanted to kiss her? Or had it all been her fault?

She shook her head in confusion. When the moment had passed, the Marquess had left her alone. She suspected that it was a hint for her to be gone before he returned to the ground floor. The least she could do was go back to Lady Ophelia and let him have his home to himself.

So she notified the footman in the hall that she was leaving for the day, with plans to return tomorrow, specifying the time of her expected arrival. Then she would see if the paper he had promised was in the library.

If he was in the house, as he had been today, she would view it as a sign that he was open to being thanked with another kiss. And who knew what might happen then?

When she returned to the dower house Lady

Ophelia was in the sitting room, reading her mail. She greeted Felicity with a broad smile, and said, 'Did you have an interesting day, my dear?'

'Yes,' she said, trying and failing to keep the flush from her cheeks. To calm herself, she added, 'The family journals are very...' She struggled for a word and decided on, 'Detailed.'

Ophelia stared at her, as if reading a detailed story of her own, then said, 'The Howell family are meticulous record-keepers. And I see the walk has put some colour in your cheeks.'

'It was nice to stretch my legs,' Felicity agreed, glad that there was an excuse for the blush that the kisses had raised.

'Did you happen to see Martin while you were there?' she asked, as if guessing the truth.

'Briefly,' Felicity admitted, hoping she would not have to make up an entire conversation to satisfy her hostess.

'We are invited to the house for dinner this evening,' the old woman said, then tapped the paper in her hand, as if eager to share its contents. 'And I have news to relay to him.'

'Good news, I hope,' Felicity said, glad of the distraction.

'We are to have an exciting month, my dear,' Ophelia said, setting the paper aside. 'Martin's mother is coming to see him.'

'Oh, dear,' Felicity said, wondering if that woman had heard of her disgrace and was coming to put her out.

'I suggested the visit several months ago and she has just now answered me,' Ophelia said, putting that theory to rest. 'I made her aware of Martin's refusal to travel to London, and his ridiculous desire to live and die without marrying, and she has come to set him straight.'

'Surely she must respect her son's judgement on that subject,' Felicity said, surprised.

'They have been giving him time to grieve—just as I have. But patience is wearing thin on all sides. It is far better that he hears the truth gently from his mother than receive an edict from his father with a list of appropriate candidates for Marchioness.'

'You do not think they will force him to make a match?' she said, alarmed for the Marquess's sake.

'He must marry someone,' Ophelia said with a nod of her head. 'There is the succession to think of.'

To Felicity it seemed that was all anyone seemed to think of, as it concerned Lord Woodley. 'He does not want to marry,' she said, since he was not there to speak for himself. 'He has the right to make his own decisions about his future.'

'Not in this,' Ophelia said, unwavering. 'He has a duty to the family and will have to yield.'

'Eventually, perhaps,' Felicity allowed. 'But not yet.'

Perhaps it was the kiss clouding her judgement, but she did not want him courting someone while she was here to see it. It would make that moment they had shared awkward.

And ensure that it would not happen again.

'He has taken long enough, my dear,' said Ophelia with a shake of her head. 'Arrangements must be made.' Then, she brightened. 'And his heart need not be involved. I think that is his real fear. He does not want to dishonour what he had with Emma.'

'That is quite noble of him,' she said, a familiar lump forming in her throat as she thought of the man's untouchable heart.

'His mother is coming to remind him that marriage need not be about love. I am sure, when she explains it to him properly, he will see the light.'

'Of course,' said Felicity, her earlier excitement deflating at the thought of the Marquess getting married. He would probably go to London, since Parliament was still in session and the Season in full swing, leaving his house here empty.

It was not as if she wanted that offer for herself. But she had been growing to like the idea of having a permanently single but conveniently kissable man living just down the road from her. It would be a shame to have him disappear just as things were getting interesting.

'Are you not feeling well, my dear?' Lady Ophelia asked, staring at her closely. 'You look paler than before. Perhaps a rest before dinner would do you good.'

'Maybe I should take a brief nap,' Felicity agreed. And if she spent her time in bed thinking of kisses, at least no one would see her blush return.

After he was sure that Felicity had left for the day, Martin went down to the library and instructed a footman to prepare the writing desk, making sure it contained the ream of paper she'd requested. As he passed the table in the foyer he ignored the outgoing mail, strangely reticent to see if she had already penned a letter to her lover on the few pages she had wheedled out of him.

He must remember that she had used him for her own ends. Never mind the fact that he had enjoyed the way she'd done it, she had manipulated him. It was not as if he had been planning to kiss her. He had merely thought her kissable. That was not the same thing at all. And now that he understood himself, he would make sure that it did not happen again.

A night of dinner and cards chaperoned by his

aunt and the vicar would make it easier to resist the charms of the lovely Miss Morgan. It would at least give him a few hours to forget how they'd spent the afternoon.

But when she arrived later she was in an evening gown that was cut dangerously low, her throat unadorned by jewellery. Could he really be blamed if he imagined ringing that neck with kisses, just where a rope of pearls might lie?

Before he could give it much thought, Ophelia breezed past the girl, presented her cheek to be kissed and announced, 'News from your mother, darling. She arrives next week.'

'I beg your pardon?' he said, as the erotic fantasy evaporated.

'She will be staying with you,' Ophelia added. 'I suspect your letter from her will be in the next post.'

'What does she want with me?' he said suspiciously.

'Cannot a woman simply want to see her son?' his aunt replied with an innocent expression.

'My mother? No.'

'She is worried about you,' Ophelia said.

'She is worried about the succession,' he corrected.

'She has reason to be,' Ophelia replied.

'And this must be the vicar,' Miss Morgan announced, perhaps trying to interrupt the old argument with the only distraction available.

Martin seized on it and left his aunt, turning to the doorway, where his other guest was waiting. 'Reverend Bainbridge, may I introduce my aunt's guest, Miss Morgan?'

'Charmed,' he said with a deep bow. 'And what brings you to Vicar's Hill, young lady?'

For a moment Miss Morgan's expression froze, her mouth still smiling but her eyes wide with panic. Then she thawed and said, 'I could say the mail coach, but in all accuracy it brought me only to the corner. I had no idea that Vicar's Hill was too small to rate a stop.'

'Miss Morgan is the granddaughter of Letitia Morgan—an old friend of mine,' said Ophelia.

'Of course,' said the vicar, then turned back to Miss Morgan. 'And how are you enjoying the country, my dear?'

She had that frozen look on her face again, and Martin wondered if she was thinking of their kiss. It would serve them both right if she blurted the truth to the vicar in a moment of weakness.

But before she could say anything, Ophelia announced, 'We shall see tomorrow, won't we?'

'Ahh, yes,' said Reverend Bainbridge with a nod. Were the two of them prescient? He had been doing his best not to think of what was liable to happen when they were alone together again. Had she told all to Ophelia?

'The Beltane Festival,' Ophelia said, giving Martin a frustrated look. 'Don't tell me you have forgotten the day again.'

'Probably because I have no intention of attending,' he replied.

'You must attend this year,' his aunt said. 'You used to enjoy it so.'

'That was...' *Before Emma died.* He'd almost said the words out loud. When he was entertaining Ophelia he tried not to speak of her, since he did not want to be a fellow who could not seem to let go of the past. But she must know what he meant.

'You are not going to make me drive myself this year,' his aunt insisted. 'Last year, I drank so much wine I could hardly handle the gig on the way back to the house.'

'You do not approve of this nonsense, do you?' Martin said, appealing to Reverend Bainbridge for help.

'It is harmless fun,' he said. 'I do not take part, of course. But the villagers enjoy it—as does your aunt.'

And if she was to be believed he needed to be there to provide a cool head and see her home safely.

'Very well...' He sighed. 'We shall all go to the May Festival, tomorrow. You as well, Miss Morgan. For if I am not allowed to bow out, neither shall you be. Let us go straight in to dinner, for we will need to make an early night of it and I want to get in several hands of cards before I send you all home.'

Felicity took the vicar's arm as they went into the dining room, relieved that Lord Woodley had chosen to escort his aunt. Much as she would have liked an excuse to touch his sleeve, seeking such things out would draw attention to her growing interest in him. She was sure she'd never hear the end of it from Lady Ophelia if the woman suspected that anything had passed between them.

At the moment that lady was occupied in describing the delights of tomorrow's festival, which seemed to involve dancing and drinking. Since all Ophelia seemed to enjoy was napping, and meddling in the lives of others, it must be a nice change of pace for her.

And it would be for the Marquess as well, should he unbend enough to partake in the festivities. But he seemed annoyed at the idea, and she wondered if he was already missing his birds.

It was too much to hope that he had been planning to meet her in the library again. He was treating her with the same icy courtesy that he had shown his aunt after the announcement of the impending visit from his mother, the Duchess. Perhaps he simply did not like change. There had been quite a bit already this week, and there was clearly more to come.

The fourth member of their party, Reverend Bainbridge, was a studious-looking man who quizzed her on her parentage and her journey from London. After her earlier reticence on the subject, he carefully avoided the reason for her visit. She wondered if he already knew the truth, or just assumed the worst about her. Which led her to wondering what the Marquess thought—particularly after the kiss.

In a way, she quite liked those assumptions. They made her seem a much more exciting person than she actually was. As far as the residents of Vicar's Hill were concerned, she was a lady with a past.

After dinner, they retired to the drawing room for a game of whist. Her three companions were pleased to have a visitor who could make up a fourth, and she suspected there would be many such card games should she remain here for any length of time. Since she enjoyed cards, it was a bright spot in a boring future.

She was paired with the Marquess, and as play progressed she was pleased to find him a smart player and a good partner. Judging by the way he looked at her when he raised his eyes from his cards, he approved of her play as well.

But the pair of them could not best the vicar and Lady Ophelia, who played like an old married couple and seemed instinctively to know the cards in each other's hands. They smiled benignly at each other, and took trick after trick as regularly as machines.

As the Marquess dealt out the next hand Felicity allowed herself a surreptitious gaze across the table, to admire more about him than his play. As she had before, she could not help but notice how much he had changed since their first meeting, and wondered what he might have been like had she seen him years ago, before his heart had been broken.

After a few hours of play the evening wound to its close and she excused herself to answer a call of nature. On the way back to the party she did not so much get lost as allow herself to wander, for she had seen a portrait gallery on the first landing of the main stairs that might give her the answer.

There, as she'd expected, was the largest and newest portrait of the Marquess and his bride. It was well placed and well lit, even though the rest of the area was dark, so it must never be far from his thoughts.

Lord Woodley's late wife had been a blonde beauty with a vivaciousness that all but leapt from the canvas. Her smile was mischievous and sparkled in her eyes, which gazed at her husband with love.

Felicity touched her own cheek, wondering what he saw when he looked at her. If this was the woman he compared all other women to he would not have spared her a moment of his time, much less a kiss, if she had not trapped him into it.

Then she looked to the painted Marquess, who gazed back at his wife with equal spirit and devotion. In the portrait, he was just as handsome as he was in person, but there was a life to him in the painting that had been almost extinguished with the loss of his family. Somehow his image seemed more real than the man himself, as if she had met and kissed a ghost.

It was a good thing she was not seeking a match with him, for there was no point in trying to capture a spirit. While he had looked at her earlier with a slow, kindling spark of desire, there was no hope of seeing the kind of devotion she saw in the picture before her. What was the point of having a husband at all if one could not have that?

It was good that she did not want a husband, she thought, giving her head a shake to clear it. Wanting to be kissed again was another matter entirely. What she wanted was a flirtation—something worthy of a woman with both a past and a future. Judging by the way he'd responded to her kiss, the Marquess might not mind something as trivial as that.

She turned away from the portrait, refusing to waste her envy on something she could never achieve, and went back to the drawing room to find Lady Ophelia in animated conversation with her nephew.

The old lady's face lit up as she entered, as if she was eager to have an ally. 'I have been encouraging Martin to throw a ball in your honour.'

'In my…?' Felicity blinked in confusion.

'And his mother's,' Ophelia added, as if a duchess could ever be an afterthought. 'It will give you both a chance to meet the local gentry. It is rare that we have two visitors here at the same time. People will welcome the excitement.' The woman smiled. 'And there will be gentlemen.'

'I really do not need…' she said weakly.

'That's what I have been telling my aunt,' the Marquess said with a frown. Apparently he was no more interested in entertaining than she was in being a source of novelty to a bunch of strangers.

'Nonsense,' his aunt said quickly. 'This is as needed for you as it is for her, Martin. You cannot stay holed up in this house with your birds. You need to be around people, and a ball will be an excellent opportunity to re-enter society.'

'But I know nothing about the organising of

such events,' he said gruffly. 'Emma would...' He stopped, as if the mention of the name caused him pain.

'We will take care of everything—won't we, Felicity?' Lady Ophelia said, beaming at her.

'Well...' She knew even less about throwing a ball than the Marquess did.

'Of course we will,' Ophelia answered for her. 'I will let you know when I have chosen a date for it, Martin.'

'Am I to have no say in what occurs in my own home?' he asked.

'I do not see why you care,' Ophelia countered. 'It is not as if your schedule changes from day to day. Nor is it likely that you will be in your hide, watching owls, on the night I choose. You will be completely free in the evening, just as you always are.'

'Well...' he said, just as Felicity had, unable to come up with an argument to counter her successfully.

'It is settled, then,' Ophelia said, smiling and looking back and forth between the two of them. 'It will make the Season far less dreary if we have something to look forward to.'

The Marquess threw his hands in the air in defeat. 'Far be it from me to stand in the way of your desires, Aunt. As long as you do not trouble me with the planning of the thing, you may use my ballroom for your entertainment.'

'And tomorrow we shall all go to the village,' Ophelia reminded them. 'You will see, Felicity, that country life is not as boring as it has been for you so far.'

Chapter Eight

The next morning Felicity came downstairs to find Ophelia had already breakfasted and was ready to leave for the village. The older woman looked at the gown and stiff pelisse she had chosen with disappointment.

'My dear,' she said with a shake of her head. 'That will not do for the first of May. You must find something lighter and more spring-like. We will be out in the sun all day, running and dancing around, and you will need the freedom of loose clothing.'

'I hadn't planned on taking part,' she said firmly. She expected to be as much of a wallflower here as she had been in London. 'I am sure if one only wants to observe...' That was what she was best at, after all.

'You most certainly will not. If I am not too stuffy to put a flower behind my ear and dance around a maypole, then neither shall you be. Now, go back upstairs and find a sprigged muslin and ask the maid to let your hair down out of those braids. I will go to the kitchen and make sure the picnic hamper is ready.' She gave Felicity one last critical look, then added, 'And loosen those stays so you can breathe. Martin is coming for us with his carriage and will be here in less than a half an hour.'

This sounded rather like her mother's advice to unbend. It led her to wonder who she was doing it for.

'If this has something to do with courting...' Felicity said cautiously.

'It is tradition. Nothing more than that,' the woman said, with an expression that was something between a plea and a command. 'The gentlemen Morris dance. The ladies dance around the maypole. Even Martin will be dancing, today.'

'Does he know that?' she asked, wondering if he was to be subjected to the same coercion.

'He will when I am finished with him,' Ophelia said with a wink.

'Then I must see this,' Felicity said with a grin, and rushed to her room to change.

Most of the clothing she had brought was elegant enough for parading down Bond Street. But at the back of the wardrobe she found an old day gown of rose-coloured muslin, with short, puffed sleeves and minimal decoration. She changed into her lightest stays and tossed it over her head, then watched in the mirror as the maid let down her hair and threaded a ribbon into it.

The transformation was surprising. She looked carefree. She felt that way, as well. The breeze from the window was fresh and inviting and she took a deep breath, catching a whiff of the lilacs in the garden.

Perhaps it might be nice to dance a bit. Just for a new experience...

She hurried down the stairs to find the Marquess waiting in the hall as the picnic hamper was loaded into the carriage. He was wearing white breeches and a linen coat, with a red ribbon tied around one of his sleeves as a sop to the day. The ensemble was a pleasant cross between the total dishevelment of his birding outfit and the elegance of his evening attire and she thoroughly approved.

She stared at him for a moment, then looked up, surprised to find that he was staring at her as well.

'Lady Ophelia told me that the event was informal,' she said nervously, when he did not look away.

'And so it is,' he replied, still staring. 'I am glad to see you are getting into the spirit of the occasion.'

'I was given no choice in the matter,' she said with a wry smile.

Ophelia appeared then, ready to shoo them both towards the door. As she had promised, there were sprigs of May flowers tucked into the braid in her hair, which she had released from its usual coronet so that it swung freely down her back. Her light dress was wildly inappropriate for a woman of her age, but the brightness of her smile made it impossible to fault her for the liberties she was taking with fashion.

'Let us go, children,' she said, gesturing towards the door. 'We do not want to miss a moment of this day.'

As Martin guided the carriage to park it next to the others lining the side of the village green, he stared out at the maypole in its centre and the bonfires that had been laid around it to be lit when the sun set. This Beltane celebration in Vicar's Hill looked much the same as the ones he had participated in as a child. After a long winter it was an excuse for the people of the area to gather and enjoy the spring.

For a change, he felt the warmth of that season in his own heart. Even though he had not been able to bear the thought of coming here last year, and no amount of wheedling from Ophelia could have changed his mind.

This year...? He was still not quite sure why he had come, but here he was. Perhaps it was the company he was keeping. Or perhaps it was that unexpected kiss.

It was embarrassing to admit that the brief interlude in the study had affected him the way it had. In fairy tales it was supposed to be the maiden who was roused with a kiss, not the hero. But there was no denying that he felt different today from the way he had yesterday. More awake. More alive. More himself than he had been in a long time.

And as the day progressed he could not stop watching Miss Morgan, who seemed changed as well. He had known she was beautiful from the first moment they'd met. But it had been a controlled loveliness, and he'd told himself that it was simply the result of London fashion and the vanity needed to maintain it.

But today she looked as she might fresh from her bed after a night of passion, with her hair loose and caressing her shoulders. The wreath of wildflowers Ophelia had placed on her head was tilted over one eye, as if daring him to come and straighten it for her.

She had been hesitant to dance at first, insisting that she had only come to watch the festivities. But when she'd seen Ophelia kick off her slippers and walk barefoot in the grass to join the circle of girls around the pole, she'd surrendered with a laugh and had gone to stand beside her.

Her cheeks were flushed now, as she wove in and out through the patterns of the dance, and the glow extended to the swell of her breasts exposed by the low neckline of her gown. Her curves were soft, her movements graceful. Her smile was inviting. She was everything anyone might want to believe about spring and blossoming youth.

The day was warm. Or was it just his blood that was heated by the circumstances? He went to the refreshment table at the edge of the green and got a mug of ale, drinking deeply and trying to gain control of himself.

He had seen women before. There were a dozen of them at least as pretty dancing about the pole as she was.

But none of them drew his attention as she did.

Because he hadn't kissed the others.

What had been awakened in him what was not some spiritual renewal. It was simply the first twinges of lust. That and this pagan celebration, which put a man in mind of finding a willing woman and a quiet place to lay her down. Somewhere nature could take its course...

He knew he should not be having such thoughts

about his aunt's guest, even if she seemed to be making an effort to lure him to sin. He drank again and turned away from her, focusing on the crowd of men around him.

'And when will we see you join us in a dance, m'lord?' asked one of the villagers with a grin.

'I came to watch,' Martin said, cocking his head towards the maypole. And only because his aunt had commanded it, he told himself. This was all Ophelia's fault.

'We have seen you dance often enough as a boy,' one old man said, with a laugh. 'Surely you have not forgotten the steps?'

'I bet he has,' said another. 'Too much time in London and at those fancy schools they sent him to. He has forgotten the old ways.'

'Certainly not!' he argued with a laugh. 'On my honour, I could dance you all into the ground if I chose to do it.'

'His honour?' said the man. 'He is a gentleman, after all. And you know how important that is to him.'

Only on a day like this would the villagers dare to mock him, as if he was still the child they remembered from summers spent with his uncle at the estate. And only on a day like this would he be willing to laugh along with them.

He held a hand to his ear. 'Is that a threat to my good name? Then I must answer to it.'

'A duel!' someone cried with a laugh. 'The Marquess must prove his word.'

The maypole dance was ending in an elegantly woven pattern of ribbons and the men were beginning to gather in rows for their dance.

'Strike up a hornpipe and we will see who the better man is,' Martin said.

If he sacrificed his pride and joined the men in a dance it would certainly take his mind off Miss Felicity Morgan. So he stripped off his coat, vest and cravat, and reached out to snatch a flower from the nearest garland, tucking it behind his ear before joining the Morris dancers.

When Felicity returned from dancing with Ophelia she went to find the Marquess, and was surprised to see him joining the other men as the music changed. He had stripped down to his shirt, and she stood transfixed for a moment at the sight of the open collar and the tight fit of his breeches as he moved.

The dance itself, with its complicated patterns of skips and stick-swinging, was rather silly, but he threw himself into it with such abandon that she could not look away. Best of all, he was smiling. It was not the polite, tight-lipped expression he wore at dinner, but a true grin—as if he could barely keep from laughing.

And then she remembered the smile he wore in the portrait with his late wife. It was the same as this. For a moment, at least, he was once again the man he had been before tragedy had scarred him.

The dance ended and he returned to them, bowing deeply as Ophelia applauded his performance. 'I did not think you'd remember,' she said.

'No one did,' he replied, accepting the glass of ale that someone handed to him. 'I trust that I have demonstrated my prowess enough for the year? And you both make delightful candidates for the May Queen.'

Ophelia laughed again. 'I am far too old for that, and glad to leave the crown to younger ladies. But for now let us eat. Cook has prepared us cold pheasant and a basket of berries, clotted cream and scones.'

'A feast,' he agreed, reaching into the hamper to spread a cloth upon the ground for them to sit.

They chatted though their picnic, stood for another dance or two, and soon the sun was near to setting and the men were coming forward to light the bonfires, handing torches to the ladies to wave while they lined up to jump over them.

The Marquess threw back the last of the ale he was drinking and rose, a determined look on his face, as the drumming and piping began again.

Instinctively, Felicity reached to hold him back. 'You don't mean to join in this foolishness, do you?'

He smiled down at her, and the firelight caught the plains of his face and made his dark eyes sparkle. 'I have joined in the rest of it. I mean to see the day through to its end.'

'Let him go,' Ophelia said, her face glowing in the warm yellow light. 'It will do him good—and it will do me good to see it.'

He left them and walked to the nearest fire. He took a running start and sailed over it, landing gracefully on the other side. Then he turned and jumped back again.

Felicity watched, amazed. The dark outline of his body against the brightness of the fire made him look like some primal god—a spirit of the season they were here to celebrate.

He was not just handsome—he was beautiful. A picture of masculine perfection.

As he jumped again, her heart jumped with him, and she felt flames licking deep within her. She wished she had the talent to draw, for she would have captured the moment to show him what he was capable of if only he'd allow himself to be happy again.

Or perhaps she would have kept the picture for herself, so she could remember this moment—

remember what it was like to be with a man so young and free.

He was walking back towards them now, still smiling, and she allowed herself to pretend that it was *her* he burned for and not just the excitement of risking himself in the fire...

The flames were burning low as they returned to the carriage, and she took the hand he offered to help her up into her seat. Was it her imagination, or did his touch linger a moment longer than it needed to before he pulled away from her and took his own place?

It didn't matter, for just the thought of it had her smiling into the darkness.

'Did you enjoy yourself, Felicity?' Lady Ophelia asked, settling into her seat and pulling a rug over her legs to keep out the night's chill.

'Very much,' she said with a sigh.

'It does the heart good to let it run wild for a bit,' Ophelia said.

'I certainly hope so,' Felicity replied, staring at the broad shoulders of the Marquess, who was sitting in the driver's seat in front of them, and wondering what the morrow would bring.

A short time later they were back at the dower house and wishing Lord Woodley a good night. Then they went off to their rooms, and the house was silent again.

Felicity lay snug in bed, thinking about the Marquess, imagining him as the hero in her current story, willing to jump through fire to save the woman he loved from a terrible fate.

She was not quite sure what that terrible fate was yet. The details would come, with a little more thought. But she was sure that the heroine was not some ethereal blonde with a permanent knowing smile. She had to be a dark-haired beauty in a rose-coloured dress with ribbons in her hair.

Suddenly there was the creak of a door opening, and the sound of footsteps slowly pacing the length of the corridor.

She froze, listening. On any other night she would have attributed the sound to a servant passing by. But the staff had been given a half-day to celebrate in the village and were either still dancing in the flames or already in their own beds, exhausted.

If not a servant, who could it be? Ophelia had already gone to her room. Even if she was up and about, her steps would have been softer and going in the opposite direction. These heavy treads sounded as if they came from a man, not a woman.

The steps were just outside her door now, and

pausing as if the being that had taken them was about to try the knob.

The hair rose on the back of her neck as she waited, barely breathing, and counted out the seconds to ten until the steps moved on down the corridor.

Was it colder than it had been before? A supernatural chill seemed to seep through the room and into her bones as she lay in bed, staring into the pitch-darkness, too frightened even to scream.

But this was ridiculous. The room was cold and dark because a fire had not been set by the servants, who were still not back from the village. If there were footsteps in the corridor, that meant there was a person there. All she had to do was open the door and call out to them and she would find out what was going on.

She forced herself from bed and slipped into a robe, shivering in the draughty room. Then she tiptoed to the door, resting her ear against the panel and listening again.

The steps were quieter now, as they moved away from her door and on down the corridor.

'Hello?' she called, opening the door a crack.

The sounds stopped again.

Now she swung the door wide open and stared out into the impenetrable darkness of the corridor. She could see nothing. The faint light from the curtained window at the end did not reach to her room, much less farther down, where the mysterious walker must be.

She held her breath and listened. Either the other person was doing the same, or...

Or perhaps he did not need to breathe.

She stepped back into her room again and shut the door, leaning against the closed panel, panting with fear.

It was nonsense, she thought, trying to calm herself. If there was a ghost it must be as frightened of her as she was of it, for it had disappeared when she had gone to look for it.

And if it was a man...?

He was probably harmless. But just in case she pushed the dressing table in front of the door to her room. Then she climbed back into bed, pulled the covers over her head and tried to sleep.

Chapter Nine

The day after Beltane, Martin sat in his hide, his sketchpad on his lap, staring at a pheasant that had come to peck in the grain he'd left as bait.

The creature was magnificent and it would be a challenge to capture the variation of its feathers—especially that long, elegant tail. That said, it was a common bird, and he hardly needed a live specimen to inspire him. He could work from the paintings he had already made, or simply go to the kitchen, where there was usually a brace of birds ready to be plucked and cooked.

And he did not really feel like drawing today. Yesterday's escapades had left him in a strange mood. A few mugs of ale and a jump through a bonfire tended to leave one feeling that the seasons would soon be changing and the impossible would become the possible.

Kissing a beautiful woman had the same effect.

He had done both in the same week. No wonder he felt restless.

His mind wandered to what might be going on in his house right now. Was Miss Morgan enjoying the writing desk in the library? What did she need to do that would require so much paper? And did it concern him?

He imagined her writing inflammatory letters to *The Times*, which amused him. More likely she was writing to a lover, as he'd first suspected, and would not welcome his interruption. Or perhaps there was more than one man in her life—hence the need for so much paper.

If she had a single special someone, then why had she kissed *him*? And why was his mind still brooding on that interlude, which had been brief and sweet and largely harmless?

Because he wanted another kiss—and perhaps a little bit more.

He had always known that some young ladies were more careless with their honour than others. Felicity's banishment to Vicar's Hill and her behaviour once she'd arrived hinted that she was none too particular about how she spent her time when around men.

She had been polite enough in the presence of the vicar at dinner, which proved she was capable of discretion, at least. And kissing him had proved she was capable of *indiscretion*, which was the sort of thing that raised a man's hopes.

Most importantly, she claimed to be uninterested in marriage and knew that he felt the same. He had promised himself that he would not wed again, but that did not have to include lifelong celibacy. Even as he had made the vow he had known that if and when a willing woman entered his life…

Of course, he had imagined someone quite different from Miss Morgan. He had assumed that if his needs grew too great to be ignored he would find a widow, or perhaps a member of the *demimonde*, and that he should return to London where such women resided. He had not thought he would fix his attention on a gently born young lady who had never wed…

And who was already dishonoured and quite possibly pregnant.

He must get the true story of her fall from grace. If she was already *enceinte*, he needn't worry about complications should things progress past a harmless dalliance and into a full-blown affair.

He allowed himself a small shudder of disapproval at the cold-blooded argument he was laying out in his campaign to heap more trouble on an already troubled girl. But it was better to be cold-blooded about this than to enter into it full of fire and passion and promises of undying love. He could not offer her that and he wouldn't pretend to.

He would hint at a few weeks of mutual pleasure and nothing more than that. In return, she would offer a yes or a shocked refusal, to which he would offer an honest apology for misconstruing her initial advances.

And as for what she was doing with all the paper he had left for her...if he wanted to know all he had to do was go and look. It was his home, after all. It should not be so far out of the ordinary for him to return to the house early, just as he had the other day. Surely, if he had fulfilled her wish, he was entitled to know what she was about?

He closed his sketchbook and slipped it into the rucksack, then headed back to the house.

Felicity sat at the writing table in the library, with a large stack of finished pages on her left and an even larger stack of blank paper on her right, pausing occasionally to close her eyes and remember the words she had written in secret, when still at home.

She had been over halfway with her story when her father had found the work, read a few pages of it, and tossed it into the fire in disgust. She could still smell the burning paper and hear his shouts as he accused her of all manner of obscenities.

For a moment the memory left her too near tears to write. Then she took a deep breath, dipped her quill in the ink and started another page.

She paused at the bottom of it to issue silent thanks to the Marquess for his help, and wondered if he would have been so co-operative had she not kissed him.

Given his choice of reading material, and his opinion on novels, he would most likely have responded as her father had—with censure and disgust. All the more reason to keep the details from him as long as she could. And that might mean she needed to kiss him again—purely as a distraction, of course.

The thought made her smile.

Then, from the hall, she heard the sound of the front door opening and the firm steps of the master of the house on his way to his study. She grabbed the finished pages and stuffed them behind a row of books, then leaned against the shelf and tried to act casual as the Marquess appeared in the doorway to the library.

He stopped, staring at her in curiosity. 'Miss Morgan...'

She smiled at him, offering a curtsey and stepping away from the books to prove there was nothing wrong. But from the look he was giving her she was only drawing further attention to herself.

'Lord Woodley,' she replied.

'How is your day?'

'Very fine, my lord,' she said, mirroring the polite smile he was giving her. 'And you, my lord?'

'Also fine,' he said, and then seemed at a loss for words.

'You are back early from your birdwatching,' she reminded him.

'Yes. Because I needed...' He stepped into the room and glanced around, as if looking for an excuse. 'A pencil,' he said, seizing one from off the table.

'Like the one you have in your pocket?' She pointed.

He looked down, as if surprised. 'Much like that, yes.'

'And now you have two,' she assured him, not really wanting him to go back to his birds, but unsure of what she would do with him now that he was here.

'Are you making good use of the paper I have left for you?' he asked, glancing at the desk, where only one half-finished page remained.

She stepped forward to block his view. 'Yes, my lord.'

'What is it that you are writing?' he asked, moving towards the desk and staring over her shoulder.

'Just notes on the family history,' she said, leaning back to sit on the edge of the desktop to hide the paper.

'How many notes are you intending to take?' he asked with a doubtful smile. 'Yesterday you were quite frantic for writing materials. You said you needed reams of paper.'

'And today I have them,' she said, then added, 'Thanks to you, of course.'

'Because you kissed me,' he reminded her.

'You kissed me as well,' she countered.

'About that...' he began, then paused as if trying to gather his thoughts.

'Yes?' she said in an encouraging tone.

'I want you to know that it meant...it *means*... nothing. Well, not exactly nothing.' He began again. 'As I told you, I have no intention of marrying you, or anyone else.'

'Nor do I,' she reminded him. 'Want to marry you, that is.'

'Not even to gain a title?' he asked, clearly surprised. 'For if I do marry...'

'Which you do not wish to,' she reminded him.

'There is the matter of the succession...'

'As your aunt keeps telling me,' she finished for

him. 'It is nothing personal, I assure you. But I am quite sure that marriage will not allow me the freedom I wish for in my future. A title might only make things more difficult. There would be obligations attached to being a duchess, I am sure. And you would want a woman with a reputation above reproach.'

'That is probably true,' he said.

'And even if I did wish to marry you, I would not be expecting an offer just because of a few kisses.'

'Of course not,' he said, and his expression was a strange combination of relief and disappointment. 'I am glad that we understand each other.'

'As am I,' she said, disappointed as well.

Their agreement should have finished the matter. If he had nothing more to say he should depart with his pencils and leave her to her work. But he did not move and neither did she.

'Did you enjoy it?' she asked, after what seemed like an eternity but was probably only a few seconds.

'What?' he asked, confused.

'The kissing.'

'It was…unexpected,' he admitted.

'So you did not enjoy it?' she said, crestfallen.

'I did not say that,' he said quickly. 'It has been a long time since I kissed a woman. Even longer since I have had a conversation like this.' Then he added,

'And I have never had a conversation like this with a girl like you.'

'What does that mean?' she asked, not sure whether she should be flattered or insulted.

'Normally in these circumstances, if the lady is unmarried, the gentleman offers either marriage or protection.'

'Protection?' she said thoughtfully. 'Am I in danger of some kind?'

He stared at her in confusion for a moment, then repeated, 'Protection. A guarantee of money and a house, jewels and so forth. In exchange for...' He gave a gesture of his hand that implied she should understand the rest.

She didn't understand. At least not completely. For no one had ever bothered to explain to her what actually happened between a man and a woman when they were in the throes of passion.

But since she did not want to display her ignorance she gave him a knowing nod. 'I do not wish to be your mistress, either. Is it not possible to kiss and...?' She returned the incomprehensible gesture he had made to her. 'And do other things in secret, without making something so formal out of it?'

'You are offering me a clandestine liaison?' he said, shocked.

'If that is what it is called,' she said, with a smile.

She hoped that was what she wanted, for she quite liked the sound of the words he was using and was sure the adventurous spinster she wished to become would approve.

But apparently Lord Woodley did not. His mouth was moving as if he wanted to speak but was unable to find the words.

'Have I said something wrong?' she asked, worried.

It took him another moment or two, but he eventually found his speech and said, 'It is just that, if such things are discussed, it is usually the man who suggests them. And never to a woman like you.'

He was calling her a woman now, and not a wayward girl. She felt some progress had been made.

She smiled at him. 'Apparently, I am not the kind of woman you think I am.'

'On the contrary,' he said. 'I think I know exactly who you are. It is just that I have never met anyone like you before.'

'I am going to take that as a compliment,' she said, smiling at him and hoping it was.

He smiled back at her. Then he turned and walked across the room, closed and locked the door. He stood with his back against the wood for a moment, staring at her in a way that made her stomach flutter with expectation. Then he walked slowly towards her, stripping off his coat and tossing it on a chair.

She swallowed nervously, trying not to stare. In London, she had never seen any gentleman without a waistcoat, and it had been rare to see one without a cravat. But Lord Woodley spent far more time out of such garments than he did in them. It was most educational.

She thought of him as he had looked in the firelight. He looked even better now, for he was staring at her with the same determined expression he'd had just before jumping.

She stared back at him, afraid to look into his eyes. Instead she focused on how very white his shirt was, compared to the tanned vee of his exposed throat. She could imagine the feel of the linen warmed by the skin beneath it. The thought made her palms tingle, and she planted them flat against the surface of the desk to keep herself from reaching for him.

'You are not having second thoughts, are you?' he asked, closing the distance between them and touching a curl at the side of her face. 'Because if you are I will not do this.'

He bent his head to her and nipped her throat.

'Or this.'

Another nip, this time on her shoulder.

'Or this.'

Now his tongue traced the neckline of her gown in one slow lick.

It was even more exciting than the kisses yesterday had been. Felicity swayed into him, eager to see what would happen next.

He chuckled at her response, and slipped an arm around her waist, pulling her off the desk and tightly to him.

'From the first moment I saw you I wondered about you,' he said, leaning close to whisper in her ear before taking the lobe between his teeth and giving it a gentle tug.

'About what?' she replied in a shaky voice.

'About how your lips would taste,' he said, trailing small kisses along her cheekbone and squeezing her hip.

'Then taste me,' she said, turning her head to try and capture his mouth.

He laughed again. 'Perhaps I shall. Later. After I have kissed you for a while.'

This was confusing, for he seemed to be talking about tasting something other than her mouth. But then his lips were on hers again and she couldn't think clearly any more. One of his hands was still on her bottom and the other was resting on her breast, as if to prove how well it fitted into his palm. And all the while he was kissing her open mouth, with little nips at her tongue that made her nipples tighten and her knees tremble. There was something about the thrust of his tongue that made her insides feel as good as her outside, and she did not want it to stop.

To encourage him, she tried to imitate what he was doing to her, kissing and nipping and touching him in return, and was rewarded by his low growl of satisfaction. The sound made her tremble even more. An answering vibration was rising up at the centre of her being, urging her on towards an unknown destination.

As if he felt her weakening, he pushed her back, then scooped her up to sit her on the writing desk. His hand trailed down her leg, stroking the outside of her thigh and reaching lower to raise her hem.

A fleeting thought crossed her mind that she should ask for some further information before they continued. She was quite sure that when her mother had suggested she be less standoffish around possible suitors she had not meant behaviour like this.

But then she remembered that she did not want to be married, so there was little reason to save her virtue. And, since she was still not totally sure what constituted virtue, how would she even miss it?

All she knew for sure was that the Marquess was

still kissing her, and doing a thorough job of it, while his hand was creeping up the inside of her leg.

'Vixen…' he muttered, his hand now clasping her thigh. 'You really have no concern for your reputation, do you?'

'I am growing rather used to being ruined,' she said with a shrug, planting a kiss at the base of his throat.

His skin was a marvel, all bristly and rough even though she was sure that he must have shaved that morning. She brushed her fingers against his cheek, noting how different it was from her own, and wondering what other differences she would note if only she undid just a few buttons and stroked his chest.

'If you are already ruined,' he said, smiling against her skin, 'then there can be no harm in my doing this…'

And his hand moved the rest of the way up her leg until there was nowhere else for it to go but—

She gasped.

The sensation of his hand on her was like nothing she'd ever felt before. No wonder they did not write about it in books, for there were no words. Even if there were, if innocent girls learned such things existed there would soon be no virtue left in England to lose.

His fingers continued to move, stroking and teasing, while his other hand eased a breast out of her bodice. Then his teeth closed on her nipple, giving it a possessive tug before suckling on it.

She rested her palms on the desk behind her and leaned back, letting him bend over her, his clever fingers doing things to her that she had not imagined were possible.

'Please...' she whispered, for she was sure that something was about to happen. Something she had been waiting for her whole life. 'Please...'

Then, after a strong pull on her breast, she felt herself parted as he thrust a finger into her, and out, and in again.

'Wait... No... Yes... What...? Oh!'

And then she knew. Oh, yes, she knew.

When she was able to catch her breath again she opened her eyes to find him staring at her.

'Are you finished?' he asked with a smile.

'I have no idea!' she gasped. 'What has just happened to me? And how do I know if it is over?'

Chapter Ten

Martin pulled his hand out from under her skirt, the hem of which was still so high that it revealed a pair of very attractive thighs in sheer white stockings.

He forced himself to look up into her face, which was almost worse, smiling as it was above one exposed breast still wet with his kisses.

'What do you mean, you don't know what has happened?' he said urgently. 'I thought you said you were ruined.'

'I am,' she said, smiling sweetly and swinging her stockinged legs. 'Just not in that way.'

'What other way is there?' he asked, backing away to put some distance between them before something even worse happened.

She looked down at her bodice and tugged it back into place with a shrug. 'I wrote a novel,' she admitted, hopping down off the desk and letting her hem fall back into place.

He blinked at her, baffled. But his body was not the least bit confused. He was still hard as a rock.

He stepped behind the chair that held his coat, hoping to conceal the embarrassing bulge in his breeches, and gave her a nervous smile. 'And what is so ruinous about that?'

'Nothing—I thought. My name was not associated with the book. When I published it, I made sure to conceal my identity. The cover said it was written by "A Lady". But my father discovered what I had done, and he says I will be quite unmarriageable should anyone find out the truth.'

'And so your parents sent you here,' he said, still puzzled.

'It was worse than that,' she complained. 'I was hard at work on a sequel. I had written several hundred pages when Father found it.' She paused, her lip trembling. 'He threw it on the fire. And he told your aunt that I was to have no paper. To prevent me from taking it up again. Clean country air and solitude were supposed to purge the idea from my head.'

'And have they?' he asked, honestly curious.

'I find it is even easier to plot here,' she said with an excited smile. 'As there is nothing to distract me.'

'Nothing to distract you…?' he repeated, dazed.

'Well, almost nothing,' she said, her smile becoming a conspiratorial grin. 'That is why I was so eager for you to give me the paper. With your help I am rewriting the story, and I hope to submit it to my publisher in secret. He will buy the copyright, since I will not have the money to publish it myself.' She gave him a thoughtful look. 'Unless you would be willing to lend me a few hundred pounds?'

'You want a loan?' he said, shocked.

'I could pay you back,' she said hurriedly. 'After the second novel was published—and for the cost of the paper as well.'

'That is not the issue,' he said. 'I just don't know if I want to be associated with your downfall when your plan goes wrong.'

'You were quite willing to assist me in my ruin just a few moments ago,' she reminded him.

'I never intended to ruin you,' he said, the guilt of what he had done warring with his arousal. 'I thought… Well, never mind what I thought. Why did you lead me to believe that you knew more than you did?'

'When have I ever claimed to have knowledge of anything?' she asked.

It was a good question. Running his mind back through their interactions, he asked himself what she had said to make him believe that she was anything less than an innocent. He had come to that conclusion all on his own, imagining a past for her that would make his actions of today if not honourable, then at least understandable.

'*You* wanted a liaison,' he spluttered, wishing that mitigated his sin.

'I still do,' she replied. 'There is no point in saving myself for a marriage which will never occur. And I assume I am correct in believing that we have done nothing so far that would result in me getting with child?'

'Of course not,' he said. 'To do that I would have to—' He stopped, afraid to give her more ideas than she already had.

'Then what harm has been done?' she said, in a reasonable tone.

It was a thoroughly masculine line of reasoning, and he did not know how to answer it. 'You really know nothing?'

'No more than what you have taught me so far,' she said with a glint in her eye.

He paced away from her, throwing himself down on the sofa by the fire, his head in his hands. He had ruined an innocent. Not completely, perhaps. But past the point where he could simply walk away and leave her.

'Miss Morgan,' he said in a hoarse voice, raising his head to look at her.

'I think after what has just happened you should

call me Felicity,' she said with a smile. 'At least when we are alone.'

'Felicity...' He began again. 'Would you do me the honour...?'

She held up her hand to stop him. 'Martin,' she said. 'May I call you Martin?'

He gave her a feeble nod.

'You are about to offer for me. And I am sorry, but I refuse.'

'But... You cannot,' he insisted.

'You do not love me, do you?' she asked. 'Be honest.'

'We have a certain...compatibility,' he said, for even as he looked at her the blood was still pounding in his loins. 'But it would be premature to call such a thing love.'

'Even if I wanted to marry, I'd refuse to even consider a man who does not love me,' she said, with a sad shake of her head. 'I am not the wife for you, Martin. You are still mourning your loss, and not ready to wed again. And I wish to support myself with my writing.'

'You would not need to,' he said.

'But I want to,' she replied. 'And it is clear that you do not understand that any more than my parents do.' She thought for a moment. 'If you wish, however, you may court me while your mother is here.

Then, later, we can declare ourselves unsuited and move on with our lives.'

It was actually a rather good idea. If he could give his aunt and mother hope, only to dash it later, perhaps they would leave him alone.

Then he looked at Miss Morgan, standing near the window with the sun shining on her hair and a delicate flush on her cheeks, and once again he was hard and ready.

'I think… No, I am sure…it will be the best for both of us if we are not alone together again,' he said.

'Why ever not?' she asked, smiling sweetly.

'It is a question of self-control,' he said. 'Mine is not what it should be.'

'I have a solution for that as well. There is no reason why we cannot carry on a discreet affair, just as we planned,' she replied.

'No reason?' He laughed. 'You cannot think of one?'

'As I keep telling you, I do not wish to marry. And, according to my father, my honour was already forfeit when I came to Shropshire. Why would a little dabbling make a difference?'

He cleared his throat. 'When I began to "dabble", as you put it, I thought you were already with child. It is not possible to get a woman in that condition when she is already there.'

'I see,' she said.

'Of course, there are ways to avoid a pregnancy and still take pleasure in each other's company,' he said—and immediately regretted the notion.

'What are they?' she asked, walking across the room and taking a seat beside him.

'I can't believe I am having this conversation,' he said, sliding down the sofa to put some distance between them.

'Why?'

'It is indelicate. Especially when speaking with an innocent young lady.'

'*Someone* must have these conversations with us,' she said with a laugh. 'We cannot remain ignorant for ever.'

'On the contrary, I think you can,' he said, leaning back and making a shooing gesture with his arms.

With an exasperated sigh, she leaned past his gesture and kissed him on the lips.

He sighed too, and then leaned into her—for her kisses were too sweet and it had been so long.

But he must resist.

He pulled away and grabbed her firmly by the shoulders to keep her at a distance. 'This is the problem with our situation. I have gone too long in solitude, and you are far too willing to fall. It is a dangerous combination.'

'But a little danger can be exciting,' she said, in a soft, coaxing voice. 'That is why you jumped over the fire last night. And why my books sell so well. They thrill without doing any harm. And just now you described a similar situation.'

'Eh?' he said, confused.

'A way to take pleasure that will not leave me with child,' she prompted. 'I am sure it has something to do with you touching me as you did before. That was most illuminating.'

'Illuminating?' he said numbly.

He supposed it was an apt description, since she seemed to glow with excitement as she leaned into him again.

'Do you feel something similar if I touch you?' she asked, staring down into his lap.

'That is not something I am prepared to discuss,' he said through gritted teeth.

'Then I will just have to find out for myself,' she said, and dropped her hand below his waist, grasping him gently between the legs.

He jumped in shock. 'I do not think—'

'It is probably for the best that you don't,' she said, rubbing her palm against him, then undoing the buttons on the flap of his breeches. 'When you touched me there was nothing between us. So I assume I must remove all obstacles.'

She pushed his clothing out of the way and stared down at him.

His member sprang up, embarrassingly erect, as if it had a mind of its own.

She looked at it in surprise, and then back to him. 'I know on an academic level that men and women are differently made. You can learn much from art,' she said. 'But I never imagined this.'

Then, she reached out and ran a finger down the length of him.

'Dear God...' he said in a shaky voice. He felt light-headed—probably from the sudden loss of blood to his brain.

'I am not hurting you, am I?' she asked, running her finger back down to the nest of hair at the root.

'No,' he said, afraid even to breathe.

'How about now?' she said, slipping her fingers around the girth of him.

He could feel himself growing in her hand...longer, wider and harder...his body readying for release.

She paused.

'Don't stop,' he said, giving up.

It was far past time for that. He no longer cared about her honour or his vows, only the feeling of sweet release that was moments away. His hands clenched at his sides for a moment, and then he reached out to touch her breast again, spreading his fingers so he could feel her heart beating under his hand. He could feel her nipple as well, hidden by her gown but hard as a pebble against his palm. He teased it out of the bodice again, pinching it between his thumb and forefinger.

She gasped and her hand tightened on him, moving from root to tip with torturous slowness.

He fished in his pocket, producing a handkerchief, and wrapped his hand around hers, guiding her to be rougher, more vigorous, harder, tighter, as desire coiled in him like a wound spring.

And then, in the moment of release, he lurched forward to take her nipple into his mouth for an equally rough kiss as his seed spilled into the handkerchief in an explosion of lust and relief.

After a few more enthusiastically grateful kisses to her breast he began to come to his senses, carefully manoeuvring her back into her gown and doing up his breeches.

'We should not have done that,' he said automatically.

'That was not what you said while I was doing it,' she reminded him.

'I should not be taking advantage of you,' he said, shaking his head.

'On the contrary. I think today it was I who took advantage of you,' she said. 'I am still intact.'

'What a horrible way to describe it,' he said, shaking his head.

'It was not I who came up with that term,' she said with a smile. 'I am still so new to this that I do not know what part of me could be broken. But I suspect you have experienced what just happened before. It is not as if I have deflowered you.'

'Well...' He paused for a moment, then finished, 'Of course not.'

'Then, as I said before, there is no harm done,' she said, still smiling. 'Now, as to the matter of my continuing to write here...'

'You did not do that in exchange?' he said, staring at her, appalled.

'Of course not,' she said. 'But if you tell anyone what I am doing I shall not do this again.'

'You shall not do it again in any case,' he said, trying to regain control of the situation.

'If that is what you really want,' she said.

But they both knew that, should the situation occur again, he would not refuse her.

'I have no intention of telling anyone anything,' he said. 'Not about the writing. And certainly not about this afternoon's escapade.'

'Escapade...' she said, as if tasting the word.

And despite his plan to have nothing more to do with her, he could feel himself getting hard again.

'You called it a liaison before,' she reminded him. 'I think I prefer that.'

'What is the difference?'

'To me, a liaison implies a longer duration,' she explained. 'And I am going to be here for several weeks at least.'

'My mother will be here in a week,' he reminded her.

'Then we don't have much time,' she said. 'We must use it well. I am expected back at Lady Ophelia's for tea in half an hour. But I will be here tomorrow at the usual time,' she said, straightening her dress. 'If you discover that there might be a way to pass the time you will know where to find me.'

Then she let herself out.

Martin sat where he was, watching her departure, still in shock. Never in his life had he met a woman so brazen. He would never have suspected that a virgin would have the capacity to do what Felicity Morgan had done to him.

He waited until he heard the front door close, then headed towards his room, stopping, as always, in the portrait gallery to stare in confusion into the face of his late wife.

And as always she beamed down at him, her eyes full of love and amusement.

'You would not be giving me that look if you had seen what just happened,' he muttered.

How would anyone have seen through a locked door? the voice in his head asked him.

And he had been the one who had locked it, planning for an outcome just like the one that had occurred. Why was he so surprised that something had happened?

'I thought I would be...'

In control?

And he had been—at least at first. And then everything had gone pear-shaped.

'She joked that she had not deflowered me,' he said in disgust.

Might as well have done.

It had been three long years since he'd known any touch but his own, and he had not expected that to change today.

'In any case, it will not happen again,' he said firmly.

She was his responsibility, since she was on his property. That meant it was up to him to guard her honour and protect her from the sort of man who might take advantage of her thirst for knowledge.

To this, the only response in his mind was raucous laughter.

He sighed and closed his eyes. She would come

tomorrow. And he would find himself back at the house earlier than expected. And he would lock the door and let the day take them where it would.

She had said that what they had done would do no real harm to anyone. His servants were discreet, and knew enough to respect his privacy, so there was no question of them being discovered.

His mother would be here in little more than a week. Their love-play would end with the arrival of the Duchess. It would be far too difficult to keep their secret after that. And when Miss Morgan left Shropshire no one need suspect something had happened and question her honour.

For a moment, thoughts of other things they might do flooded his mind. Visions of lips on bare skin and hands touching everywhere...a frenzy of exploration resulting in an earthshattering mutual climax.

'Madness,' he said, pushing the thoughts away. Self-indulgence and the desire to be handled by her again. He must be on his guard against temptation and go back to the way he had been before, living in scholarly chastity.

Why?

That was an excellent question. Though he did not think he could love again, declaring himself celibate was another matter entirely. He had always assumed that a woman would eventually appear and tempt him enough to take that step.

His only objection to the one who had come was that she was inexperienced. It was clear that she did not intend to stay, so why should he not be her first lover? It was not as if she needed to save herself for marriage, as she had made it clear that she wished to support herself and had no desire for a husband.

Most importantly, she would have no plans to marry *him*. He could not have found a better lover if he'd made one up out of his imagination.

He looked at the painting with a sheepish shrug, and Emma looked back at him, still amused.

'It is decided, then,' he said. 'A brief affair. Nothing that might lead to marriage or a child. And then life will go back to the way it was.'

If you say so.

The words echoed in his confused mind as he walked the rest of the way up the stairs.

The afternoon had been a revelation.

That was the only way Felicity could think to describe what had happened between her and the Marquess.

Martin, she thought, and smiled. She would call him that, at least in the chaos of her own thoughts.

My dear Martin. Oh, yes, please. Again, Martin.

She sighed as she imagined what might happen between them. For after the brief anatomy lesson he had given her, she suspected she now knew what occurred when a man and a woman were alone together.

At least when they were alone and in love.

Not that she was in love with Martin, she told herself firmly. She did not think he would like it if she fell fully in love with him. That would hint at permanence and marriage and all the other things she had promised him she would never ask for or expect.

She was probably just infatuated.

She liked the sound of that word. It was rather like the word *intoxicated*—full of bubbles and giggles—and there was a strange, expectant tingling in her body, as if it knew there were great things in store for it.

She was infatuated with Martin the Marquess. She grinned, wishing there was someone with whom she could share the truth. But she could hardly announce to Lady Ophelia what she had done, and she dared not write down the details for fear the wrong person would read it.

She would have to keep the secret quietly, next to her heart, no matter how much she wanted to sing it out. And if some of what she felt found its way into her book, heavily disguised by fiction, then who would know?

Though she did her best, she could not help the smile on her face when she arrived back at the dower house, and nor could she hide her glee from Lady Ophelia.

'Did you have a good day, dear?' the old lady asked, giving her a searching look.

'Yes, very,' she replied, searching for a lie. 'My walk was most invigorating. And I saw so many animals. A fox with kits, and in the distance a stag.'

'Birds as well, I suppose?' Ophelia said, with a knowing smile.

'Of course,' she agreed, doing her best to control a guilty start. 'I do not know the names of them.'

'You must talk to Martin about that,' Ophelia urged gently. 'I am sure he would be happy to discuss them with you.'

'I imagine he would,' she said.

Perhaps the next time they were together she should ask him about his studies. Then, when Ophelia questioned her about their interactions, she would have something to say other than the exciting truth.

But for now she sipped the tea that her hostess had poured for her and held her tongue.

Chapter Eleven

The next day Martin spent the morning in his hide, trying to pretend that he was not imagining an afternoon with the delightful Miss Morgan, doing things that would make the vicar blush.

It was one thing to consider an affair with her and another to let such thoughts rule his life or ruin his studies. He was still in control and had made no promises to her. He could stay in the woods and draw all day. He could resist this if he wished to.

But instead he went back to the house just after lunch, locked the library door and lost himself in her arms.

Today, their lovemaking was a rush of passionate kisses, rumpled clothing, flashes of skin and whispered words, ending in shuddering mutual satisfaction. The fact that they stopped just short of consummation made the whole thing even more erotic.

It was like walking on the edge of a cliff, knowing that at any moment they might fall.

But for her sake he would not let them. He had promised her and himself that there would be nothing between them that might lead to a child, and he meant to keep his promise.

Despite what she'd said, he could not quite believe her insistence that she would never marry. To live on the profits from writing prurient fiction was the stuff of fantasy. She would need a husband at some point—someone who could support her. And that lucky man would want to be sure his children were his own.

For his part, he wanted no unfortunate emotional entanglements. All the pleasure but none of the pain he associated with love. Being with her would be like having a mistress, and yet not the same thing at all.

Unlike with a normal mistress, he would not need to ply her with flowers and jewellery. All she wanted was more paper. Even now, when she was lying in his arms on the library sofa, her eyes had strayed to the desk and the pile of finished pages, as if she might leave him at any moment and go back to work.

He frowned. It was not that he was jealous, exactly. But he was curious as to what it was about the work that obsessed her so.

When she released him, and sat up to straighten

her clothing, he rose and went to the desk to take a look at what she had been working on.

As he reached for the top sheet he heard a sharp intake of breath.

He turned to find her rushing across the room, reaching to take the paper from his hand.

To placate her, he set it back on the desk and said, 'After what we have done to each other, I had not expected to find you shy about your writing.'

'It is not finished yet,' she said, reaching past him to gather the day's work and sliding it behind a row of books on one of the shelves, hiding it like a squirrel with a nut.

'And when it is done? Will you let me read it then?'

'Have you read my first book?' she asked, folding her arms in front of her chest and standing guard between him and her precious manuscript.

'Of course not,' he said. 'I do not read novels.'

'Then why would you want to read this?'

It was an excellent question. 'I am curious as to what all the fuss is about,' he admitted. 'What could you have written that shocked your parents into sending you from town?'

'My first book was called *The Mad Monk of Montenero*,' she said with a proud smile, as if she expected him to recognise the title.

He stared at her, baffled.

'*The Times* called it "a salacious tale of murder and mayhem".' At the thought she smiled, as if such a review was the highest compliment she could have received. 'It was quite successful,' she added. 'The sequel shall be *The Abbey of Montenero*.'

'Where the mad monk came from?' he asked, trying not to laugh.

'Exactly,' she said, warming to the subject. 'You see, the mad monk has a long-lost sister named Columbina, who is searching for him. She falls into the clutches of the abbot, who holds her prisoner in one of the cells...'

'I see,' he said, annoyed to find her almost as excited by these imaginary people as she had been by his lovemaking.

'But Columbina has a suitor who was turned down by her father for being honest, but poor.'

'He doesn't like honesty?'

'Well, he was the one who sent his son off to be a monk...'

'Which drove him mad?' Martin supplied.

'Actually, it was the ghost of the weeping nun that did that.' She smiled. 'Really, it all makes more sense if you have read the first book.'

'Of course,' he said, secure in the knowledge that such a thing would never happen.

'I saved up my allowance for a year to afford the

first printing, and I made a tidy profit—even after Mr Ransom, the publisher, took his share.'

'And what happened to the money?' he asked, assuming she had run through it as fast as it had come to her.

Her smile faded. 'My father found it in my room and took it all. It was not a fortune. But it was enough to let me live independently of my parents. They would hear none of that. They said I must marry. My mother told me that I'd had no offers because I was too lackadaisical in my responses to interested gentlemen.'

'Lackadaisical?' he said, thinking of how eagerly she had received him just now.

She nodded. 'But really I think it is that I do not find them as interesting as the men I make up.'

It was exactly what he'd feared. 'Real men are not the stuff of gothic heroes,' he said. 'Nor are they as villainous as your mad monk.'

'I am aware of the fact. The problem is not that I seek perfection. It is that I fear most gentlemen would be like my parents and disapprove of their wives writing books,' she said with a firm smile. 'I have yet to find a man who seems willing to make allowances for my planned career. I thought it best not to encourage the few suitors who appeared, as they would only stand in the way of my goals.'

'Sensible, I suppose,' he said, not convinced.

'That is why we get along so perfectly together,' she said, beaming at him. 'We will not even be able to maintain what we have for more than a few days, much less agree to a marriage that neither one of us wants.'

'A few days?' he said, surprised.

'When your mother is here these visits will have to stop,' she said, and had the grace to look disappointed. 'There is no way we could keep such a thing secret.'

'You are probably right,' he said, stunned by the practicality of her mind. 'If my mother sees us together she will have us down the aisle before either of us know what's what.'

'And I suppose I shall have to find another place to work as well,' she said, a trace of wistfulness creeping into her voice.

She was thinking of the book again, and it annoyed him. When he had been young and single he had been secure in the knowledge that with looks, money and a title he could have any girl he wanted. He had never expected to meet a woman who would refuse him out of hand because she wanted something more than the honour of being his wife.

And now she cared more about the future of her writing than she did about the end of their affair.

'Where will you work?' he asked, unable to keep the mockery from his tone. 'Do not worry. I will make sure that you can finish your blasted novel. As long as I do not have the read the thing when you are through. It sounds dreadful.'

Her eyes narrowed as the barb hit home. 'I wouldn't dream of making you stoop so low,' she snapped, in an equally sarcastic voice.

He stared at her for a moment, transfixed by the anger flashing in her eyes and the pout of her full lips. If possible, she was even more beautiful than she had been before. Heat was sizzling between them now, and he felt the desire to make her forget her imaginary lovers and think only of him.

'Since we will have so little time together, we must make good use of the few days we have left,' he said, and grabbed her hand, pulling her roughly to him.

And then her lips were on his and nothing else mattered.

They made love again. Or at least something like it. Martin had assured her that what they were doing was a pale imitation of the act, which he had described in detail, whispering the words into her ear to inflame her passion as he fondled her.

Even though she was annoyed with him, it did not seem to affect the way she felt when he touched her.

If anything, their play was even more exciting than it had been earlier in the day, frantic and almost rough.

When it was over, she saw the triumphant, possessive look in his eyes and wondered what it was that he felt he'd proved to her.

Could it be that he was jealous of her writing?

She watched him through lidded eyes as they made themselves presentable. He was tucking his shirt into his breeches, his stance wide and arms crooked, as if he meant to take up all the space in the room and leave no room for anything but him.

He looked masterful.

A few moments ago, when she'd been in the mood to be mastered, his arrogance had worked to both their advantages. Now she was not sure what she wanted from him.

She felt almost relieved when he slipped into his birding coat and unlocked the door, giving her a parting smile and promising that they would meet tomorrow.

Now that he was gone she could go back to work.

But as she stared at the blank page his comment echoed in her mind.

'It sounds dreadful.'

Did it really? Her parents seemed to think so, as well. And, if she was honest with herself, those reviews in the newspapers had been nothing to brag about. But they had not bothered her the way this most recent criticism did.

Perhaps it was because she felt so strongly about him. Martin was not just handsome, exciting and rich. He was intelligent and cultured as well. And, despite his attempts to be otherwise, she found him charming. Really, he was as close to perfect as a man could be.

When he had asked about her writing she'd been flattered that he was interested, and had hoped, just for a moment, that she had been wrong about what men expected from women. She had thought that just maybe he might tell her that a man who truly loved her would be impressed by what she had achieved and would cheer her on to greater heights. Who knew what she might do in the future if, along with love, she found a husband who did not think she was a foolish girl with an embarrassing hobby?

But instead Martin had proved what she already knew. He'd dismissed her work without a second thought, unable to accept that she might have any interest other than him. It was for the best that their relationship would not last beyond the week, for they could have no future together.

But why did the truth depress her, so? Had she lived so long on fantasies that she could not accept the reality that was right in front of her? He did not want to marry and neither did she. This was the happy ending to their story. They would both get exactly what they'd planned for.

She glanced at the desk again and sighed. Since she could not think of anything but Martin, and his blunt assessment of her story, there was no point in remaining here. She would return to the dower house and hope that tomorrow would find them both in a better humour.

On his way to his room Martin stopped in front of the painting, wanting to vent his frustration on someone who would not argue with him.

'She is driving me mad,' he muttered, staring into Emma's beautiful blue eyes, which had not caused him a moment's pain while she'd lived.

So soon?

He had known her for less than a week and their intimacy could be measured in hours.

'Long enough to know the truth,' he said.

At first sight?

'She is nothing like you,' he said, remembering how quickly he had fallen in love with Emma. 'The situation is totally different.'

You are different as well.

'Older and wiser,' he said.

And more cruel.

He had behaved like a spoiled child when confronted with Felicity's excitement over her work. He could have kept his opinion to himself, but had not been able to resist provoking her.

Her hobby did no real harm to anyone—especially not to him. He must find a way to make it up to her when he saw her tomorrow.

Lost in thought, he continued up the stairs to his room.

When she returned to the great house the next day Martin was waiting for her in the library, with no trace of yesterday's irritation in his manner.

'Get your bonnet and come outside with me. I want to show you something,' he said, smiling.

'What?' she replied, curious.

He did not answer, but led her out of the house and then kept on walking towards the main road for half a mile, before cutting into the field, his strides widening, forcing her to hurry to catch up.

'Where are we going?' she asked, panting with exertion.

'To my hide,' he said, smiling with pride.

'Has anyone else seen the place?' she asked.

'No one until now,' he said, heading towards a cluster of trees in the middle of the field.

She smiled and hurried after him. He had not told

her he was sorry in so many words. But she did not think he would share this intimate part of his life with her just so they might argue in private.

They passed several clumps of trees before coming upon a small wooden shack, with slitted windows along all sides and a door at the back. He reached for the leather handle and swung it wide, gesturing for her to enter.

She walked inside and waited as her eyes adjusted to the dim light coming through the tiny windows and the cracks in the walls. The interior contained a small stool near the front, a table in the centre of the room, and a cot placed against the back wall.

She looked at him, surprised. 'Why do you have a bed here?'

'Because it is so peaceful that I sometimes enjoy a nap in the afternoon,' he admitted. 'No one ever comes here, you see. They know I would not like the interruption for it might scare my birds.'

'Am I likely to scare the birds away?' she asked.

'Not so that I will notice,' he said with a smile. 'I did not bring you here to watch birds, you see.'

She smiled expectantly.

And then he produced a pile of paper and a small inkwell from the rucksack he was carrying. 'If you wish to continue your work while my mother is visiting, you may come here and get the privacy you need.'

'Here?' she said, shocked.

'I doubt I will be able to use the space, as my mother will monopolise my time,' he replied. 'And she would ask too many questions if you were working in my library. But my space here is yours to use for as long as you need it.'

It was a generous offer—especially from a man who had no particular interest in her work.

She reached out and gave him a hug of thanks. 'This will suit me well,' she said.

'You will have no interruptions. I do not think my aunt even knows where this place is, much less wants to visit it. And my mother...' He grimaced. 'She will not venture from the house without several footmen and a well-sprung carriage.'

'No distractions at all,' she said with a happy sigh. 'That is just what I need to complete my book.'

He might not want to read it, but he cared about what made her happy and was willing to accommodate her. That was almost as good.

'You may work now, if you like,' he said, pulling the table close so she might sit on the cot to write. Then he pulled out a notebook. 'I can continue with my observations as well. And perhaps later, when we need a break from our labours...'

He pulled a bottle of wine from the bag and glanced from her to the cot.

'That sounds delightful,' she said.

Then she sat down, sharpened a quill and set to work.

Martin picked up his spyglass and stared at the nearest tree, scanning each branch from top to bottom. Even when he did not find anything new or interesting a feeling of tranquillity stole over him when he was here. It was the only place he felt truly at peace.

He had expected the presence of another person in the little room would ruin that. Instead, having Felicity here with him seemed to calm him even further. There was something very comfortable about them working together on their respective projects, and her quill scratching against the paper and the soft sound of her breathing blended with the usual birdsong, becoming a pleasant accent rather than a distraction.

A happily shared silence was not something he had experienced when he had lived with Emma. With her, there had been bustle and noise almost continually, and much laughter. While he had loved the life he'd shared with her, he'd never had time to sit in the woods, alone with his thoughts, as he did now. She'd have laughed at him for it, and insisted he come back to the house to keep her company.

But Felicity was different. She seemed to understand the studious part of him almost better than he did himself, and she accepted it without question, fitting into his private space like a puzzle piece dropping into its rightful spot.

This train of thought surprised him. It was almost as if he thought they might belong together for longer than a week. He did not dare to tell her that—for what did he have to offer other than a relationship that would lead to public ruin should it be discovered?

And, although she would probably laugh at the idea of becoming his mistress, he did not think she really wished to court scandal to such a degree.

He put away the spyglass and turned to her.

She looked up from her work and smiled. Then she put down her quill and said something no other human being had said to him before.

'Tell me about your wife.'

The request shocked him, for it was the last thing he'd expected to hear from a woman he'd made love to. But he had come to realise that Felicity Morgan was not just any woman. She was a continual source of surprise.

He crossed the room and sat down beside her on

the bed, reaching to fold her in his arms and wondering if she sought reassurance that she was currently the most important person in his life.

But perhaps he was the one who needed comfort.

He wanted to speak, but did she truly want to hear?

She held him as he was holding her, stroking his hair until he laid his head on her shoulder and began.

'She was more full of life than anyone I had ever met. She had the voice of an angel, and when we danced it was like walking on air. From the first moment I met her, I knew.'

'Love at first sight?' Felicity murmured.

He thought of his conversations with the painting and nodded. 'I did not believe in it until it happened to me,' he said.

'It is nice to know that such a thing exists outside of books,' she replied.

When he looked up at her face she was smiling, as if she could share his happiness without a hint of jealousy.

'It was real,' he said. 'As the months passed our love never wavered. And then...' His voice faltered.

'You lost her,' she finished for him.

'It was so sudden,' he said, remembering that night, surprised that he could speak of it without tears. 'We had such hope. We were going to be a family. I waited in the corridor for the sound of the baby's first cry. But all I heard was Emma's screams of pain. And then silence.'

'How awful,' she said.

He felt her arms tighten about his waist and it gave him strength to continue.

'Perhaps it would have been easier if I had been able to say goodbye,' he said, then added, 'Sometimes I talk to her portrait. There, she looks the way I like to remember her.'

Not cold and pale and still, as she had been when the surgeon had called for him.

She nodded in agreement. 'Sometimes it is easier to make up a story than to live with the full weight of the truth. I find it so, at least.'

'Is that why you write?' he asked.

She smiled. 'Perhaps it is. I have never been content with the life that I was destined to have. In my stories I can be whoever I like...go wherever I wish.'

'But for now will you be with me?' he asked, surprised at the need he felt, which was something beyond desire. He wanted the warmth of her to ease the old pains, to help him find the parts of his soul he had lost.

She nodded, and kissed him. And suddenly the

past was not nearly as important as the pleasure that could be had in the next few minutes...alone together.

Chapter Twelve

Felicity quite enjoyed the birdwatching hide. It had a tranquil atmosphere that was conducive to working. And it also had Martin. But with only two days remaining until the arrival of his mother, the Duchess, she was continually aware that their time together would be ending.

She did not know how long she might stay in Shropshire, and nor did she know how long the Duchess planned to remain. And if that woman convinced Martin to marry, he might turn away from their secret affair and never look back.

Her stomach knotted at the thought. It was foolish of her to have become so attached to what they had. She had assured him, and herself, that it would not last for ever. But that did not mean she was ready for it to end.

Nor did she want it to feel so incomplete. While

what they were doing together was delightful, her body craved a true consummation of their...

Did she dare to call it love?

In her heart, she did. There was more to what she felt than simply desire.

There was something in the melancholy nature of the man that made her soul ache to soothe him. And while she did not think he would ever forget his late wife, she wanted to see him smile again as he had in the painting.

His goal to publish his work on the local birds was, in some way, very like the path she had taken when writing her own book. He was preparing something wonderful, and she wanted to be there with him, to see him succeed.

Today, they were together in the library, for it had rained in the night and it was too wet to go into the woods. He brought his painting in from the study, working on the table as she sat at the desk.

He moved a stack of diaries from the surface, back to the shelf they'd resided on, and gave her a side-long look. 'I trust you have surrendered your search for the dower house ghost?'

'I have looked from one end of the dower house library to the other and pored over all the diaries and journals in your house as well.'

'And you have found nothing,' he said, with surprising certainty.

'I have never met a family so lacking in myth and legend,' she said, shaking her head in disgust. 'To a woman of my imagination it has been very disappointing.'

'I am sorry we could not accommodate you,' he said, coming to kiss her on the back of the neck.

'However, the phantom has been far more co-operative than the family that birthed him,' she said. 'I have heard him walking the corridors on multiple occasions.'

'You can't have done,' he said. 'There is no such thing. Ophelia told me so herself.'

'Then she was lying to you,' she answered, equally sure. 'I am getting quite tired of waking to unexplained noises in the night. It is impossible to get a good rest with something, or someone, creeping just outside my bedroom door.

'If you want the answer all you have to do is open that door and look for what causes the noises,' he said, proving far too pragmatic.

'I have done so, and seen nothing,' she said.

'Then light a candle and step into the corridor,' he suggested.

'I am too frightened to do so,' she said, embarrassed.

'Because you really think there is a ghost?' he said with a laugh.

'If there is such a thing, then it is hardly surprising that it frightens me,' she said primly.

'And if there is not?'

'Then it might be an intruder, and it would be quite beyond my ability to deal with one,' she said.

'Or it could be your imagination,' he replied. 'That is by far the most likely answer, you know. It is all loose floorboards and mice in the wainscotting.'

'Then it will be no trouble at all for you to handle it,' she said triumphantly. 'Come to my room at night and see for yourself. There must be some reason your aunt is telling me such tales. Either she is hiding something, or she honestly thinks that her home has spirits.'

'She only told you the story to keep you in your room at night,' he admitted.

'Because there is something going on that she does not want me to see,' Felicity said. 'There is something very wrong about the whole situation. I fear that her mind might be troubled in some way.'

'And that is why you are involving me?' he said. 'Because you fear for my aunt's sanity? I have not yet met a woman who is more sound in thought.'

'Aside from in this one instance,' she said.

'And you want me to sneak into the house myself

and banish the ghost?' Martin said, wrapping his arms around her and pulling her even tighter to him. 'It is not that I do not want to help you,' he said. 'But I do not know if hiding in your bedroom is wise.'

'As if we will do anything there that we have not already tried,' she said with a scoff.

But on second thoughts, the nearness of Martin and a comfortable bed was an appealing combination.

'What we have done so far is risky enough. To be alone in the night in a bedroom with you would be even worse. You are an unmarried female. But you will not be one for long if I am discovered,' he said, with a shake of his head. 'Your father—'

'Would probably be relieved that I have found something to do that is not writing,' she finished for him. 'But he is not here to force you to marry me, so we needn't worry about him. If we are caught by your aunt we will explain everything and swear her to secrecy.'

'*You* will explain,' he said, shaking his head. 'Because I am still unsure just what I would say that she is likely to believe.'

She ignored his objections and went on. 'We will wait until Ophelia goes to bed at ten tonight, and then I will come downstairs and open the door for you. You can sneak up the main stairs to my room and wait.'

'And if the phantom does not come?' he asked.

'Then I will let you back out again and no harm will be done,' she said.

'You have said that to me before,' he said.

'And you have enjoyed the results.'

'Against my better judgement. But, yes, I have.' He sighed. 'All right. I will help you hunt for your phantom. But when things go wrong, as I am sure they will, do not think to blame me.'

That night, Felicity tried to contain her excitement as she and Ophelia retired to the sitting room after dinner. Though she was normally tired, and went to bed early, tonight it seemed to take for ever for the woman to declare that it was time to retire.

As the clock crept towards ten Felicity thought of Martin, creeping towards the house only to be stranded outside. She experimented with a couple of broad yawns, trying to encourage her chaperon to sleep.

'Why don't you go to bed, dear?' the old lady said, as alert as ever. 'You seem tired.'

'Perhaps I shall,' Felicity replied, giving an elaborate stretch as she stood. 'You must be tired as well,' she said, smiling.

Ophelia blinked back at her, surprised. 'Not particularly. You go on ahead. I will follow as soon as I am finished with this sermon.' She tapped the book in her lap, apparently riveted by the subject.

Felicity smiled back at her, cursing silently to herself. Then, she went upstairs to her bedroom, opening the window wide so that she could see the shadowy figure waiting by a tree at the front of the house.

She leaned as far out of the window as she could, teetering on the sill and letting out a loud 'Psst!' to get Martin's attention.

He looked up at her, his face glowing in the faint light from the house.

'There is a problem,' she whispered.

'I can see that,' he said, gesturing to the light still shining out through the downstairs windows.

'You will have to climb up,' she said, patting the tree that grew close to her window.

'Surely you jest?' he said, his expression blank.

'It is not far,' she encouraged. 'Only twenty feet or so.'

'Straight up,' he reminded her.

'And I suspect up is easier than down,' she encouraged.

'Do you, now?' he said.

'You can use the stairs when you leave.'

His sigh of resignation was audible over the breeze. 'How kind of you to offer.'

Then he jumped for the lowest branch, hauling himself up with a grunt.

After a few minutes of rustling leaves and muttered curses he was balancing outside her window, inching out on the last branch to reach the sill.

She offered a steadying arm, pulling him into the room just as the branch dipped alarmingly under his weight.

He lurched forward, toppling them both to the ground. He lay atop her for a moment, panting, and she listened for any sign that their fall had been heard by the rest of the household. Then their eyes met. She was about to say something about the ludicrous nature of their situation, but her mind went blank and all she could see was the depths of his dark eyes, staring into hers. Their mouths were so close she could feel his breath, steadying as he relaxed into her.

'You are in your nightdress,' he said in a hoarse voice.

'I am,' she agreed, squirming under him. 'The maid would have thought it odd if I came upstairs and then did not undress for bed.'

He stood up, brushing at his coat to hide his distraction, and picking a leaf from his hair. 'After all this there had better be a ghost,' he said.

'I assure you there is something going on,' she whispered, walking to the door and putting her ear to the panel.

Then she held a finger to her lips, urging him to silence as she heard Lady Ophelia coming up the stairs.

They waited together, hardly breathing, as the old lady walked down the corridor to her room, and a while longer until they heard her maid retreating down the back stairs.

'What do we do now?' Martin asked in a whisper.

'We wait,' she said gleefully. 'The sounds normally begin after midnight, if they happen at all.'

Then she went and sat on the bed, patting the mattress at her side.

'And until that time?' he said, giving her an ironic smile.

'We will sit in the dark,' she replied, blowing out the candle.

'I see.'

He sat down next to her on the bed, his leg so close to hers that she could feel the warmth of him through the thin lawn of her nightgown.

'It is a long time until midnight,' he whispered, leaning in to brush her ear with his lips.

'Only a couple of hours now,' she said, smiling into the darkness.

'Was ghost-hunting the real reason you lured me here?' he asked with a low laugh.

'The main reason,' she said, for other possibilities *had* occurred to her.

'You must know the risk of inviting me,' he said with a sigh.

'Just as you know the risk in coming here,' she said, reaching out to him in the darkness.

'And yet I could not refuse you,' he said, slipping an arm around her waist and pulling her close.

'We do not have much time left together,' she said.

'I suppose that is true…' he agreed, absently stroking her back.

It worried her. What if he was not feeling the urgency that she felt as the hours ticked away?

'I do not want you to forget me,' she said, walking her fingers up his chest to toy with the knot of his cravat.

'That is not likely, I assure you,' he said, kissing the place where her throat met her shoulder. 'You live just down the road from me, after all.'

'For now,' she agreed.

'And we will see each other at dinner, and at that damned ball my aunt wishes to hold,' he said with a sigh.

'But we may not be alone again after tomorrow,' she reminded him.

This was met with silence. Did it mean that it pained him to speak of it, just as it did her? Or that he was not particularly bothered by the fact? Perhaps he was even looking forward to ending their meetings.

Just as she was about to question him further on the matter one of his hands moved up her ribs to rest on the underside of her breast. Then he paused for a moment, as if considering.

'What are you thinking?' she asked at last.

'That it is much nicer now that you are not wearing stays,' he said, kissing her quickly on the lips.

He was right. It was. This was the first time she had been alone with him largely unhindered by clothing, and she felt positively wicked.

'It would be even better if you were not fully dressed,' she said, and started to undo his waistcoat buttons. Then she kissed him on the mouth in a way that she hoped made clear her willingness to do anything he wanted.

He pulled away, but only for a moment. 'I am probably going to regret this...' he said, but she was still close enough to feel his smile.

He pushed her down on the bed, following to lie

beside her as his fingers slowly undid the buttons of her nightdress.

Suddenly, a loud creak sounded from the corridor. They froze.

The sound was followed by measured footsteps, passing just outside her door.

'See?' she said on a whisper. 'It is just as I told you.'

'Do up your nightgown,' he said, whispering too as he fumbled with the buttons on his waistcoat.

Then he jumped to his feet and rushed to the door, throwing it open and lunging into the corridor.

There was a scuffle that did not sound in any way supernatural, and Felicity reached to light a candle from the coals in the fireplace. Then she carried it into the corridor, to see Martin holding on to a man in a black cloak, pinning him against the opposite wall.

She held her candle up to get a better look at him, then pulled it away in shock. 'Reverend Bainbridge!'

Farther down the corridor Ophelia's door opened, and she stepped out of her room, her candle raised, to see what the hubbub was about.

'Oh, dear,' she said rushing forward. 'Are you all right?'

It was clear that she was talking to the vicar.

Martin released him, and the man looked back at her. 'No harm but to my dignity,' he said.

'I don't understand…' Felicity said, looking from one to the other of them.

'Any more than we understand what Martin is doing in your room at this hour, dear,' Ophelia replied in a prim tone.

'I am here to investigate the matter of the haunting,' Martin said, giving her a sceptical look.

'Perhaps you should have asked me, instead of going to such lengths,' his aunt said.

'And what would you have told me?' he asked.

'That it was none of your business,' she said, in a disgusted voice. 'And now perhaps the vicar should see you out, and I will have a talk with Miss Morgan.'

That gentleman could not seem to decide whether to look affronted or sheepish at this dismissal, but in the end he turned in silent agreement and headed towards the stairs. A short time later Felicity could hear the front door open and close again.

When they were alone, Ophelia looked at her and said, 'If the hour was not so late I would call for tea. But I do not want to disturb the servants. I have a small flask of brandy and a pair of glasses in my room that will serve just as well in the way of refreshment.'

She led the way back to her room and poured out a small glass for each of them as Felicity lit candles and poked the fire back into life. Then she went to sit in one of the armchairs by the fireplace and waited nervously for the scolding she feared was coming.

Ophelia handed her a glass, and Felicity sniffed it cautiously. She had never drunk spirits before. But tonight seemed to call for something stronger than wine and she accepted it gratefully, then sipped carefully so as not to choke.

After drinking herself, and more deeply, Ophelia began. 'I am sure you must be wondering why the Reverend Bainbridge was sneaking into my room at night.'

'I would not presume...' said Felicity, with a cautious shake of her head.

'Do not be silly,' the older woman responded. 'I must tell you that it is exactly as it looks. We have an arrangement that I did not want to forgo for the duration of your visit. But neither did I want to tell you the truth.'

'So you made up a story of ghosts to keep me in my room?' Felicity said with a smile.

'It seemed a harmless ruse. But it did not occur to me that you would brood on the subject enough to haunt the halls yourself.'

'I nearly caught him the other night,' she admitted.

'I am aware,' Ophelia replied. 'Poor Geoffrey stayed in the corridor for nearly an hour before coming to my room.'

'Wouldn't it be easier, if you wish to continue keeping company, for you to marry?' Felicity asked.

'For some, perhaps,' she said. 'But we are both quite comfortable with our lives as they are. I do not want to move to the parsonage, and it would hardly be appropriate for him to stay here. If I marry out of the family they will not allow me the dower house. And this house and the freedom I've found in widowhood are the only advantages I gained from my union with my late husband Charles. We were not particularly happy as a couple, and nor were we blessed with children.'

'How sad that you were left alone,' Felicity said automatically.

'But that is just it. I am not alone. I have Martin, who is very much like a son to me. And Geoffrey for company...' She smiled. 'My life is just as I want it to be. And I am more than just content, I am happy.'

Felicity nodded, for this proved just what she'd always expected. For some women it was better to remain unmarried.

Then Ophelia added, 'It is not as if either of us is young enough to start a family—which you must admit is a primary consideration when entering into a marriage.' She gave Felicity a searching look. 'Avoiding children is also important, if one means to avoid marriage.'

'I suppose you are right,' Felicity said, staring at the floor.

'I believe we have now established that I am the worst chaperon your parents could have chosen,' Ophelia said with a shrug.

'Not at all,' Felicity assured her. 'It was not fair of my parents to impose on you and to expect you to change your habits for my sake.'

'Well, it is too late to do anything about it now,' Ophelia said, taking another sip of her drink. 'Just as it is probably too late for me to lecture you about the dangers of being unchaperoned with a gentleman, and what might occur if you are not careful.'

'Tonight was all my fault,' Felicity said firmly. 'I talked the Marquess into coming here and I do not expect him to offer for me. At least, not if he doesn't want to,' she added.

For she was not quite sure what she wanted any more when it concerned Martin.

'You are aware that he does not wish to marry again? Do not delude yourself into thinking he will change, unless he gives you reason to,' Ophelia said firmly. 'That way lies heartbreak, and I hope to spare you that, at least.'

'I do not want to marry either,' Felicity said, trying to sound like the confident confirmed spinster she'd planned to be. 'Martin is allowing me to write in his house. And when I finish my next book I will sell it and have the money to live on my own terms.'

'Which you will have to should you accidentally fall pregnant,' Ophelia said bluntly. 'Have you given any thought to that?'

'We have done nothing, as yet, to risk that,' she said cautiously. Then admitted, 'At least I think we have not. But I have questions about the process.'

Ophelia nodded. 'And it is better that someone educate you instead of letting you blunder on in ignorance. I will pour us another drink and tell you whatever you want to know.'

Martin had left the dower house with the vicar and they walked in silence down the road for several minutes before the other man spoke.

'I hope you do not think less of your aunt because of tonight's discovery.'

'I do not know what to think,' Martin admitted, for he could not decide whether to be stunned by the discovery, or by the fact that he had been discovered himself.

'Ophelia and I have an understanding,' said Reverend Bainbridge.

'And the less I know about it, the better,' Martin finished for him.

'And you and Miss Morgan...?' the vicar said, leaving the rest of the question unspoken.

'We have done nothing that would prevent her from making a decent marriage,' he said.

'Some would say otherwise,' Bainbridge replied, giving him a sidelong glance.

'You think I should offer for her?' Martin said, speaking the thought that had been nagging at him for some days.

What they had meant as a playful interlude was growing into something he was not sure he understood.

'I am in no position to lecture you on that point,' the vicar said, and they walked on for a time without speaking.

'It would not be fair to her if I could not give her my whole heart,' Martin said at last. 'And she is adamant that she does not wish to marry at all. She wants to make her own way in the world and live off the profits from writing gothic novels.'

'Is such a thing feasible?' Bainbridge asked, clearly surprised.

'I have no idea,' Martin replied.

'Well, then...' The vicar cleared his throat. 'I

would suggest that you be careful, and do the right thing should something unfortunate occur.'

'Of course,' said Martin. 'I will do nothing to risk her future or her happiness.'

Even if it meant losing his own.

They had reached the turning for the drive to the main house and Martin stepped off the main road to go home.

'Good evening to you, sir.'

'And to you as well,' the vicar said, giving him a final worried look. Then he continued down the road towards the village.

Chapter Thirteen

Her discussion with Lady Ophelia had been very informative. By the time Felicity went to bed she understood the cause of pregnancy, and the precautions normally taken to avoid it.

It was just the sort of talk she'd hoped to have had with her mother. But that woman would have been horrified by her curiosity, and would probably have preferred that she discover things through trial and error on her wedding night.

And apparently there were hard truths to learn.

Though she'd not have thought so, after her time with Martin, Ophelia had told her that the act itself was sometimes painful, or unpleasant—especially if one's first time was with a man who was clumsy or inconsiderate. She had said that with some men there might be no pleasure at all, for they thought of nothing but their own needs in the bedroom.

Felicity wondered if the old lady had been trying

to scare her with this, for it certainly sounded awful.
But after some consideration she decided that it was
just a solid reason to make sure her first time happened with a man she already trusted to care about
her pleasure.

And, since his mother arrived the day after tomorrow, there would not be a better time than now
to take that next step on her road to discovery with
Martin.

When he arrived at the hide, Martin was surprised
to find Felicity had arrived before him. He was even
more surprised to find her gown and petticoats hang-
ing from a nail on the wall, while she sat on the cot
completely naked.

He paused in the doorway for a moment, frozen in
place, dazzled by the sight of her. In their past meetings he had been too afraid of discovery to remove
her garments, merely lifting skirts and unbuttoning
a few buttons here and there to reveal glimpses of a
body he could only imagine.

The sight of her in her nightgown on the previous evening had revealed more than he'd ever expected to see of her, although the evening had been
spoiled by his long cold walk with the vicar, and the
reminder that he was taking risks with her honour.

Apparently she'd got a lecture of an entirely different sort. For what possessed her to be naked in broad daylight, her legs crossed in a most unladylike fashion, a bare foot tracing lazy circles in the air as she nibbled on the end of her quill before scribbling a line of text on the paper before her on the table?

'What the devil are you doing?' he whispered, his voice cracking like a nervous schoolboy's.

'Waiting for you,' she said with a brilliant smile, totally unashamed.

Or perhaps not. Was her skin always such a rosy pink? Or was she blushing from head to toe?

'You cannot...' But obviously she could. 'You should not be so exposed.'

'Why not?' she asked, giving him an innocent blink. 'Does anyone but you ever come to this place?'

'Never,' he assured her.

'Then you are the only one who will see me. And I do not mind.'

She stood and stretched her arms above her head.

He watched her breasts rise and fall with the movement.

'It is surprisingly comfortable.' She looked at him consideringly. 'You should try it.'

'I know what it feels like,' he said.

'Well?' She stepped forward into his arms, rubbing her body against the front of his coat. 'Wouldn't this feel better without clothing?'

Of course it would. That wasn't the point.

'My mother will be here tomorrow,' he reminded her.

'All the more reason to seize the day,' she said.

Then she deliberately walked away and lay down on the cot, one foot still on the ground, the other leg bent at the knee, giving him more than a glimpse of paradise.

'We cannot…' he repeated, as the last of the blood left his brain.

'Apparently we can,' she said, rolling half on her side and propping her head on one bent arm. 'There is a thing called withdrawal. It requires a certain amount of control on your part, but it sounds very interesting.'

'You should be saving that for—'

'For whom?' she interrupted. 'Are you saying I must take another lover? Because that is not your decision to make.' Now she looked faintly worried. 'How will I know if the next man is as kind and gentle as I know you will be? What if I do not enjoy it? And what if all the while it is happening I am thinking how much I regret that I did not do it with you?'

It was a good question, and one that had crossed his mind before. There was bound to be a first time for her. Suppose her lover did not care for her as he did? The thought of her responsive body and hopeful spirit in the hands of some selfish boor made his gut clench.

'I have thought about it,' she said, still smiling. 'And I want my first time to be with you.'

When he did not respond, her hand dropped into her lap. She touched herself and sighed, rolling onto her back and spreading her legs in invitation.

He watched in fascination. He could not resist. There was only one way to end the madness she was visiting upon him.

He stripped off his clothing, eager to be as naked and free as she was.

Felicity smiled up at him and stifled a sigh of relief. For a moment she had feared that he might simply laugh—tell her to put her clothes back on and return to the house. But judging by the way he was looking at her now, he wanted her just as she wanted him.

As he pulled his shirt over his head she admired the flex of his muscles and the broad planes of his chest and stomach. She held her breath as he removed his breeches and she saw the glory of him, naked and aroused.

He came to the cot and hovered over her for only a moment before covering her with his body. The feeling of skin against skin was even better than the kisses and touches they'd shared thus far, and she could not resist touching every part of him she could reach.

He caught her hands and brought them to his lips. 'You are mad to do this, you know.'

'Perhaps I am,' she said, smiling up at him. 'But I cannot be any other way when I am with you.'

He kissed her then, and nothing else mattered but the taste of him...the feel of him ravishing her mouth. Her blood pounded in time to the thrusts of his tongue and her body tightened in expectation of his claiming.

His hands gripped her hips, steadying them as he eased his manhood between her thighs. The weight of it pressing against her felt right, as if she had been waiting all her life to feel his body against hers.

He was murmuring into her ear now...soft apologies for the pain he might cause. She touched a finger to his lips to silence him, then kissed him to put their fears to rest.

He was touching her now, opening her, pressing against her. She held her breath and felt him push, an uncomfortable pressure, and then there was a feeling of such rightness and completeness that she wanted to cry.

He sighed, and stilled, letting her adjust to the

feel of him becoming a part of her. Then he began to move.

'Yes!' she cried out, unable to be silent. 'This! Yes, this...'

She moved her hips in time with his, for it seemed the right thing to do, and he rewarded her by increasing the pace and depths of his strokes, teasing her and then finding home again.

She felt the rhythm begin to change as his breathing became ragged and his muscles tightened. And then he pulled away and finished without her.

Before she could express her surprise, his hand slipped between her legs to give her what she needed—a climax which was long and sweet.

They lay together in silence for a time. She put her arms about his neck and her head against his chest, listening to him breathe.

Then he pulled away from her and sat up, staring out through the narrow windows at the world outside. He turned to her, his face dappled by the meagre sunlight that found its way in through the boards.

'Miss Felicity Morgan, would you do me the honour of becoming my wife?'

For a moment she was the happiest woman in England.

But only for a moment.

When she had first come out she had imagined the

moment of proposal much as she imagined everything—as a scene in a much longer story. The prospective groom would be smiling a little nervously, perhaps, and down on one knee. His hand would be reaching out to her as if offering the world…

But really it would not be much of the world. Only his small corner of it. And really it would only be a portion of that—for what wife truly partook in all that had been allotted to the man she married?

The man who offered for her would certainly not be offering her the eventual title of Duchess, because she would have no idea how to fulfil the role. She could not even imagine that—though she could imagine all the problems with it easily enough.

The man who offered for her would also not look as stricken as Martin did now, as if he was being forced into some horrible mistake.

He also wouldn't be naked. But that was her fault—as was the stricken look. She had tempted him into lying with her and tricked him into a proposal that he did not want to make. Though it had been her goal to make them both happy, she had made him miserable.

So she did the only thing she could think of and stood up, reaching for her clothing. 'Do not be ridiculous, Martin. Of course I will not marry you.

Haven't I made it clear enough that I am not interested in a relationship of that sort?'

Then she focused on getting dressed as best she could, making it a point not to look at him, for fear that she would see the relief on his face and burst into awkward tears.

'You do not understand the situation you are in,' he said, and she could hear him grabbing boots and breeches to make himself presentable. 'The method we employed for safety is by no means foolproof. And I cannot risk having a child born on the wrong side of the blanket.'

So this sudden change had a great deal to do with the seed of a future peer and nothing to do with his feelings for her. She could not decide if that hurt more or less.

She experimented with a laugh, to show him how little she cared for the risks. But to her ears it sounded more panicked than carefree.

'You may be worried, but I am not. It would be most annoying to realise that we had married for no reason and were stuck with each other for the rest of our lives just because of a few minutes' pleasure.'

'That was all it was to you?' he said, in a tone as sharp as breaking glass.

'That is all it can be,' she reminded him, struggling into her stays and turning her back so he would

help her with the laces. 'Your mother arrives tomorrow, does she not?'

'And when she does, Ophelia will tell her what has
been going on and we will be wed before the week
is out,' he said, his words punctuated by sharp tugs
on the laces at her back.

'Ophelia will say nothing,' she assured him. 'I
spoke to her last night, after you and the vicar went
away. She understands that forcing a couple to marry
is not the best solution to every problem.'

'Even without Ophelia's interference I should—'

She cut him off. 'I have no interest in being part
of your supposed obligation. I will not be here much
longer, and I did not want to miss my last opportunity to be with you. But once I have finished with
this book I will be gone, and you will not have to
bother with me any more.' She hesitated, then said,
'I am sure you will be glad to get rid of me.'

This was the point where he should argue that
her time here was not a burden to be borne, but at
the very least a memory to be cherished for the rest
of his life.

Instead, he muttered, 'I have been neglecting my
work. There are drawings back at the house that I
wish to finish. I will have no time after tomorrow—
for them or for you.'

It was a blunt truth, but she was relieved he had admitted it.

'You had best go back to them, then. I will remain here, for I have at least ten pages left to write today. From now on I will come in the afternoons to work on my book. If you do not wish to be bothered with me...'

'I will come in the mornings to study,' he finished. 'And now, if you will excuse me, I will be on my way.'

'Of course,' she said, holding her breath until he was well out of earshot and she could burst into tears.

He had been an idiot.

Martin marched at a quick pace away from the hide and back to the road, stumbling over a rut and allowing himself a hearty curse that had nothing to do with his stubbed toe.

She had seduced him and, like a fool, he had let her. And then she had not allowed him to do what was obviously the right thing—especially if they wanted to continue doing what they had been.

He arrived back at the house and slammed the front door on the way in—which was probably a mistake if he did not want the entire staff to know he was at home, and then see him in the portrait gallery, yet again, talking to the only woman who could not answer him back.

He stared up at Emma, who looked more amused than usual at the state he was in.

'The woman is clearly mad,' he said, not bothering to explain that he'd made a further slide downwards on his slow fall from grace.

She's not the only one.

'I offered and she refused me. Didn't she realise what an honour I had presented her with?'

How romantic.

He winced, for that the statement had made him sound like a pompous ass.

'She thought I could forget all about her.'

As if that would be possible after what they had done together.

And you said you were going back to your birds.

He hadn't meant that he preferred the birds to her company. He had just been so shocked at her refusal that he'd wanted to get away and lick his wounds like a whipped dog.

What are you going to do now?

'I have no idea,' he whispered to himself.

If he marched back to the hide and tried to start again she would probably repeat her refusal. She'd made it clear that she was going to finish her book and leave.

And after tomorrow he would have his mother to deal with, and secrets to keep that were more likely to be revealed if he spent too much time in proximity to Felicity Morgan. Perhaps it was best if, for the moment, he stayed away from her just as he'd said he would.

Chapter Fourteen

After an uneasy night Martin rose early. He had his valet dress him in his finest day coat and tie a cravat so stiff and snowy that it would have made Beau Brummell weep with envy. No matter how unwelcome it was, he meant to give his mother's visit the respect it deserved. And that meant his birding clothes must be banished to the back of his wardrobe until she had gone.

After a light breakfast he went to his study to compile his notes on the week's sightings, desperate for anything that would make him forget yesterday's abrupt finish to his love affair.

They had both known that it had to end. But he had imagined something more sweet than bitter... something not nearly as intimate as it had been. He could not shake the vision of her naked body striped with sunlight, like a gift wrapped in gold ribbon.

And her love had been a gift—though she'd

claimed to offer it for selfish reasons. Then she'd taken it away again, just as suddenly.

At last he heard a carriage pulling up in the drive, and shook himself from his reverie to go and greet the Duchess. She was just entering as he arrived in the hall, and he bent to offer her a polite kiss on the cheek.

'Mother,' he said respectfully.

'Martin,' she responded, giving him a head-to-toe look and frowning with disapproval.

'How was your trip?' he asked.

She sighed. 'Tedious, as always. The least you could do, Martin, is settle in London, so visiting you is not such a chore.'

'Someone must manage this property,' he said with a shrug.

'But not year-round. Be honest and admit that the place would do just as well under an overseer or a steward.'

'Or I can remain where I am and do it myself,' he said, with a firm smile.

'Until such time as you wish to remarry,' she said. 'And you will not find a wife sitting here.'

'I am not looking for one,' he said, hoping the events of yesterday were not in some way visible on his face.

'If you are not, then I will be forced to help you

do so,' she replied, removing her bonnet and walking towards the sitting room.

He signalled for tea to be brought and moved ahead of her, opening the door and seeing her seated comfortably. Then he replied, 'I do not need your help in managing my life.'

'I beg to differ,' she said, reaching into her reticule and removing a folded sheet of paper. 'I have taken the time to prepare a list of appropriate young women who would be good candidates for Duchess.'

'You are choosing your eventual replacement?' he said with a laugh.

'If you do not, someone must,' she said, unfolding the list.

'I thought I had made it clear that I have no intention of remarrying,' he said.

'On the contrary, your exact words when Emma died were that you would never love again,' she replied. 'Perhaps you do not understand the fact—for your experience was limited to one year—but marriage and love need have nothing to do with each other.'

'You wish me to spend the rest of my life with someone I do not love?'

'I wish you to wed and procreate,' she said in a merciless tone. 'Neither of those things will take a lifetime. In fact, they will take very little of your time. Once you have done them, you and your wife can live separately and do as you please.'

Or he could marry someone he desired, whose company he enjoyed, and spend the rest of his days with her.

What had he said or done that had made Felicity refuse? And why must he think of that now? These were the sorts of questions that he would rather share with the painting. At least Emma did not take offence if he tried to live his life as he saw fit.

He cleared his throat. 'If it will not take much time, then there is no reason to hurry the decision.'

He had rushed into enough things lately, without his mother's encouragement. Hopefully Felicity was right that his aunt would not enumerate his mistakes over the next family dinner.

'Ophelia says she is entertaining a young lady from London,' his mother announced.

He gave a guilty start. 'Miss Felicity Morgan.'

'Is she of good family?' she asked, but did not wait for an answer. 'We will have them to dinner tonight and I will meet the girl and see for myself.'

'Do not think, just because she is female and unmarried, that I should make an offer for her,' he said.

At least not twice in two days.

'Of course not.' His mother smiled. 'As I said, I

have not met her yet and cannot make a judgement. But Ophelia is quite impressed by her.'

He sighed. 'She has made me aware of that fact.' He stood up. 'Why don't you let Mrs Spang show you to your room, and we will discuss it all later?'

Ad infinitum, he was sure.

'While I am resting you will issue the dinner invitation to Ophelia and her guest,' her mother said, in a voice that made the evening meal sound like a command from the King.

'Very well,' he said, without enthusiasm.

If his mother insisted on meeting Felicity, they might as well get it over with. Then perhaps the Duchess would lose interest and leave the poor girl alone—just as he should have done.

Felicity dipped her quill in the inkwell and scribbled a last line on the page in front of her, before setting it aside and cracking her knuckles, trying to work the cramp from her hand.

It had been an exceptionally productive day, with twenty pages finished. The climactic scene was approaching, and in a week, more or less, the lovers would be united, the villain vanquished, and the ghost laid to rest.

Would that her own life could be as easily managed.

Now that she had stopped writing, and was not

caught up in the story, she was painfully aware of the silence in the hide and the fact that, although she had arrived earlier than promised, Martin had not been there to greet her. Was he busy with his mother? Or was he simply avoiding her?

If he was, she did not blame him, for she had probably wounded his pride with her refusal. But even though she had been up half the night, debating the matter with herself, she did not regret her decision, only the handling of it. She should not have hurt him.

Of course, he should not have had the look of a man facing the gallows when he'd asked her to be his wife. But she told herself firmly that he had not broken her heart with his obvious distaste for a union with her. If she was to be a carefree woman of the world she must not spend time weeping over a failed affair.

Not that this affair had failed, precisely. It had all been going quite well before he'd spoiled it by proving that he did not love her. Or perhaps it was her mistake for falling in love with him. She had not planned to do so. She had been sure that she'd wanted nothing more than the physical pleasure he was so adept at giving her.

But if that had been true she would not be missing him now, wishing that he could be here with her, even if it was just so she could watch him as he watched his birds. She missed the sound of his voice, his dry sense of humour, and the sight of his hands holding a pencil as he sketched his subjects.

She rose from her work and made her way back to the dower house, favouring Ophelia with a wan smile as the woman asked her if she'd enjoyed the walk she'd told her she was going to take.

'It is a fine day,' she said automatically. 'Most fine indeed.'

'And did you happen to pass the Duchess's carriage on the road?' Ophelia asked.

Of course she hadn't. She had been hidden in the woods and absorbed in her work.

'I stopped in a field and took a nap beneath a tree,' she improvised. 'It must have passed by while I slept.'

Ophelia gave a disappointed shake of her head, as if judging the inferior quality of her lies. Then she said, 'You will have opportunity enough to meet the Duchess later. Martin has sent us a note, requesting we go for supper.'

'I did not expect to meet her so soon,' she said, trying to hide her discomposure.

More importantly, she hadn't expected to see Martin again. How were they going to sit across the table from each other without revealing all that had happened in the last few days? He was probably still angry with her. And she…? She was afraid that his mother would take one look at her and read her sins on her face, as clearly written as on the pages of one of her books.

Ophelia gave her a worried smile. 'You have nothing to fear from Martin's mother. She can be a tyrant, and she is used to getting her way. She will probably be short-tempered after her trip. But other than that it will be no different from meeting any other exceptionally difficult person.'

To Felicity, that sounded like more than enough reason to be frightened. 'I have never dined with a duchess before,' she said.

'But you have dined with a marquess, and that is almost the same thing,' Ophelia assured her.

'But that was just Martin,' she replied.

'I would recommend that in his mother's presence you call him Lord Woodley,' Ophelia corrected her gently.

'Of course,' Felicity said in a weak voice.

'Go upstairs now, and have a wash and a rest. Then… Your blue dinner gown, I think. It is modest, but most becoming. And perhaps for the occasion I will lend you my pearls.'

'That is most kind of you,' she said, and went upstairs to prepare for dinner.

When they arrived at the great house Martin was there in the hall, waiting to greet them.

Felicity gave him a nervous smile and said, 'Lord Woodley, thank you so much for the invitation.'

Was it her imagination, or did he give a slight flinch at the sound of his title on her lips?

'My pleasure, Miss Morgan. And Aunt Ophelia. It is good to have company.'

'Other than the company you already have?' his aunt said in a subdued tone.

It seemed he could not help grinning back at her. 'It has been a long day. If you are here to enumerate my flaws, you are too late. It has already been done.'

Ophelia responded with a knowing nod. 'Fear not, Martin. We are here to provide a diversion.'

He led them into the sitting room, where his mother was already waiting.

'Mother, may I introduce Miss Felicity Morgan?' he said, stepping aside and leaving her standing in front of the Duchess.

She dropped into a curtsey and murmured, 'Your Grace...'

The older woman lifted a quizzing glass from the

ribbon at her wrist and stared through it at her, making her feel like an insect in a bell-jar.

'Miss Morgan,' she said with a dismissive nod. 'Who are your parents?'

'Mr John Morgan of London,' she said with another bob. 'And my mother is named Maryanne.'

'Hmmm…' the Duchess said. 'Who are your mother's people?' she asked, clearly still puzzling over her.

'The Winstons, also of London,' Felicity said. 'I doubt you would know them.'

'Of course not,' the Duchess said with a dismissive shake of her head.

'I knew her grandmother when we were at school,' Ophelia supplied, by way of giving her pedigree. 'Miss Cassingdale's Seminary for Young Ladies.'

The Duchess raised one eyebrow and stared at her sister-in-law, as if to say that she neither knew of nor cared for the place.

'And you, Miss Morgan?' The quizzing glass swung back to examine her again. 'Did you attend this school?'

'I was educated at home, Your Grace,' she said, wondering if this was a strike against her or a point in her favour.

'That is always preferable to boarding, if one's parents can hire the right sort of tutors. You learned languages, I suppose? French, Greek, Italian?'

'No, Your Grace,' she admitted.

She'd never before felt her education was lacking. But now she was not so sure.

'I learned a bit of Latin. But I fail to see the point for I've had no reason to use it.'

'Hmph.'

By the sound of it, she had answered wrongly again.

'If you are finished with interrogating our guests, Mother, it is time to go in to dinner,' Martin said, clapping his hands as if to break the Duchess's train of thought and offering his arm to his mother to escort her from the room.

Felicity fell into step behind them and took a place on the left side of the table, next to Lady Ophelia. It put her across the table from the Duchess, who was still looking at her with interest as the first course arrived.

'What brings you to Shropshire, Miss Morgan?'

'My parents thought a stay in the country would be good for my health,' she lied, and then let out a weak cough to hint at a disability of the lungs.

The Duchess was not impressed. 'In the middle of the Season?'

'Yes. Well...' Felicity said with a shrug, and coughed again.

'Were your parents aware that my son would be

in residence, just down the road?' she asked, giving Felicity a critical look.

'I do not think so, Your Grace,' she replied, trying to focus on the soup that was being ladled into her bowl.

'Really, Mother,' Martin said in a tired voice. 'I am hardly a reason that parents might send their daughters to Vicar's Hill.'

'Then what *is* the reason?' his mother countered. 'Everyone who is anyone is in town until Parliament ends. I would be in London myself if I were not here to shake you out of your reclusive behaviour.' She looked at Felicity again and said, 'Surely you would rather be dancing at Almack's than keeping company with an elderly lady in the country?'

'After several Seasons out, I am on the shelf, Your Grace,' she said with a forced smile. 'It is not so bad keeping company with Lady Ophelia.'

'And my son,' the Duchess said with narrowed eyes.

'He has been most gracious in his hospitality,' she said, wishing that Martin would contribute something to change the direction of the lady's thoughts.

'Miss Morgan is a fine card player and a welcome addition to our social set,' he agreed. 'Perhaps, while you are here, we can gather enough people to have a small card party.'

'We are throwing a ball as well,' Ophelia added. 'A chance for you and Miss Morgan to meet the neighbours.'

'I see...' the Duchess said in a knowing voice, as if she saw far more than they'd meant to show her. 'Miss Morgan, do you think that the odds of a match might be better now you are outside of London, where no one knows of your past?'

'My past?' The words came out in a guilty squeak.

'There must be a reason you have not found a husband,' the Duchess said, giving her another direct stare. 'You are pretty enough...and have decent manners. Your parentage is nothing to speak of, of course. But...'

'Mother!' Martin said with an appalled expression.

'I speak nothing but the truth,' his mother said, unbothered.

'It is quite all right,' Felicity lied, trying not to let her annoyance show. 'There is a perfectly logical reason I have not made a match, Your Grace. It is because I have no interest in marrying—here or in London.'

'You do not wish to marry?' the Duchess said, her eyebrows raised. 'And how will you manage without a husband? What do your parents think of such a plan?'

'My parents do not approve,' she admitted honestly. 'They have sent me here in part because of my disobedient nature. As for managing…' She smiled. 'I am quite capable of making my own way in the world.'

'Miss Morgan is an authoress,' Martin said, before the Duchess could question her further.

Felicity glared at him, for she had hoped to keep her plans a secret, to avoid the scorn that her profession seemed to evoke in most people.

But the Duchess nodded in understanding, then looked to Martin. 'Many young girls go through a similar phase. I, myself, toyed with writing before I met your father.' She turned to look at Felicity. 'Once I found a husband I came to my senses.'

'And that is why I do not wish to marry,' Felicity said, looking from one of them to the other, and then back to the Duchess. 'I have already published my first novel and am now working on a sequel.'

'I have been allowing her to work on it in my library,' Martin added, 'since she is forbidden to work on it while under Aunt Ophelia's care.'

'I gave my word,' Ophelia reminded them.

'But I did not give mine,' Martin replied, in a tone that brooked no opposition. 'You had nothing to do with this, Aunt, and cannot be blamed for what comes of it.'

'You are encouraging the writing of novels?' his

mother said with a horrified expression. 'The next thing we know you will be reading them.'

'Certainly not,' Martin replied, as if she'd suggested he might walk naked through Hyde Park. 'All I am doing is providing paper and a desk. That does not make me a patron. It is not as if I am providing for her welfare.'

'I should certainly hope not,' his mother replied. 'If you mean to keep a woman do it for the ordinary reasons—not to promote dubious works of fiction by some feminine quill-driver.'

'Mother...' he said in a warning tone.

'That is quite all right,' Felicity said again, with a firm smile. 'Your mother is entitled to her opinion.'

'How gracious of you,' the Duchess snapped.

She was being rude, and Felicity knew her mother would have been appalled. If her mother had been here she'd have scolded her into silence or found a way to send her from the room.

Of course, her mother had never met a duchess—much less dined with one. And, judging by the way this evening was going, Felicity doubted that she would be invited again. She might as well go on as she was and continue to stand up for herself.

'I am sorry to appear so recalcitrant,' she said. 'But I have done what I have done and it does not matter who shames me for it. I would not take it back even if I could.' She smiled. 'In fact, I enjoy it.'

'As long as you do not mean to read it to us I suppose there is no harm,' the Duchess replied.

'Of course not,' she said with a brittle smile. 'And if you are worried that I might be angling for the Marquess you should take consolation from my plan to continue my career. There is no way he would want to marry a woman with such a disreputable habit.

'That is true,' the Duchess replied, brightening.

And if Martin remained silent, only Felicity noticed it.

After what seemed like the longest dinner of Martin's life, Ophelia and Felicity gave him their thanks and departed, leaving him alone with his mother again.

He turned to her in exasperation. 'You were rude in your treatment of Miss Morgan.'

'I did nothing more than say what people in London are probably thinking,' she replied.

'Since she published anonymously, the truth of her hobby is not widely known,' he said.

'If it was supposed to be a secret, why did you announce it at the dinner table?' she asked.

He'd wondered the same thing as soon as the

words had come out of his mouth. Perhaps he had done it because, after her refusal yesterday, he'd wished to hurt her, as she'd hurt him.

'I should not have done,' he said, then added, 'Just as you should not have attacked her. If you mean to treat all young women that way you need not worry about me remarrying, for there will be no one willing to accept me.'

'Nonsense,' his mother snapped. 'They will simply be required to stand up to me—just as Miss Morgan did.'

'That is true,' he said, surprised by the rush of pride he felt on her behalf. 'But in the future you will stop harassing her, or I will put you in your carriage and send you back to Norfolk.'

His threat was met with a noise of disapproval and a look that made him wonder if his mother saw the truth better than he did himself.

Before she could give any further response, he bade her goodnight and went to his room.

'Well, that could have gone better,' Ophelia admitted, as the carriage drove them the short distance back to the dower house.

'I don't see how,' Felicity said, remembering the scorn that the Duchess had displayed towards her even before she'd learned of her books. 'Would she have been any kinder to another woman? Someone from the first tier of society?'

'Probably not,' the old woman replied. 'If you were already a duchess, or perhaps one of the few women who outrank her, she might have been more polite.'

'But then she would not have seen me as a threat to her son,' Felicity said. 'How did she treat Martin's late wife?'

'Abysmally, when she was alive. She has risen in the Duchess's estimation now that she has had the good sense to die tragically,' Ophelia said with a sigh.

'That is often the way of things,' Felicity said. 'The next Marchioness will be compared to the first and will always be found wanting. That is true for both the Duchess and her son.'

'Perhaps not so much for Martin,' Ophelia said. 'At present he fears that will be the truth. But he does not know enough about love to understand how malleable it can be—and how resilient the heart is if it is given a chance. When he finds the right woman he might love even more strongly and deeply than he did before.'

'Or he could simply marry for duty and feel nothing,' Felicity said, unconvinced.

She should not have voiced that opinion, because Ophelia was now looking at her curiously, probably wondering if she had some information on the subject that she was not sharing.

She turned to the window and stared out into the darkness for the rest of the journey.

Chapter Fifteen

He should never have allowed her to kiss him.

That thought occurred to Martin more than once in the coming days, as he did his best to avoid Miss Morgan and everything that reminded him of her.

But that was almost impossible. She had been in the country for little more than two weeks, yet she seemed to have marked each corner of his life in a way that left her ever-present in his mind.

Here, she had come in through the door with a hopeful smile.

There, she had dined, sparring with his mother and wearing a gown that exposed her elegant throat.

There, she had played cards, with the light from the fire bringing out the chestnut in her dark hair.

And in the study, she had kissed him.

That memory made it almost impossible for him to work there. And as for the library... He could hardly go into the room. The same went for the hide, where he could still feel her naked body, warm and willing under his.

'I am glad you have given up that nonsense about birds,' his mother said, clearly having noticed that he had not been out for his daily observations.

'I have not given it up,' he snapped. 'I am merely taking a pause from my work to spend time with you.'

His mother laughed—a short bark that cut through the silence of the house and made the sparrows just outside the breakfast room window take flight.

'When did you begin to care about my feelings, Martin? Perhaps you think I will be lonely out of your sight for a few hours. I assure you that I am quite capable of entertaining myself, should you wish to go back to staring morosely at some poor feathered creature instead of staring morosely into space at nothing.'

'I am not...' he began, but then worried that her description might be accurate.

'You think I am here to force you to marry, so that the succession will be secured,' his mother said with a scoff. 'But perhaps I have come because I do not wish my only son to wallow for ever in misery over a thing that he cannot change.'

'I am not wallowing,' he insisted, wondering if that was indeed what he had been doing.

Before Felicity had arrived he had spent many hours thinking of Emma and wondering what life would have been like had she been able to share it with him. Now his time seemed filled with longings for a live woman, instead of a dead one. He was not sure if this new obsession was an improvement.

'Here,' he said at last. 'I will show you what has been occupying my time.'

He walked to the study and returned with his portfolio, stuffed with paintings neatly arranged and separated by tissue, ready for the day he might take them to the printer.

His mother paged through them, making small favourable noises which were an improvement over her usual annoyed *hmph*s.

When she reached the end of them, she looked up and asked, 'Is this all?'

'All?' he said, incredulous. 'That is every species that can be found in the area.'

'More than that,' she replied. 'There are duplicates. I can see three greenfinches, at least.'

'The colour was not always quite right,' he said defensively.

'The colours are near to identical,' she corrected. 'Have you shown them to other ornithologists and asked their opinion? Your similarly obsessed friends, perhaps?'

'I have no…' He stopped.

Was he really about to admit that there was no one in his acquaintance with whom he talked—about this or anything else?

No one but Felicity, at least. He had opened his heart to her just the other day. But even after all they had shared he had not shown his work to her.

'Perhaps there is an ornithological society in London,' his mother said, giving him a speculative look. 'A visit there is in order.'

'I will go when I am ready,' he said, refusing to be goaded.

'Then go back to your birds now,' she said with a shooing gesture. 'The quicker you complete the project, the sooner you can move on with your life.'

'I will do that,' he said tartly. 'If only to get away from you for a few hours.'

Felicity bit her lip in concentration as she filled another page, blotting it and setting it with the ever-growing stack of finished work. There was something about her current state of mind that spurred the creative process, making it even easier for her to write scenes of poor Columbina's incarceration and longing for her lost love.

Perhaps she was taking her own misery and confusion and putting it into the book. She had not seen

Martin since the night of their dinner with the Duchess. It had been three long days since then, and she grew to miss him more with each passing minute.

But what was she to do if she saw him again?

She could not decide whether she wanted to throw herself into his arms or upbraid him for making her writing a topic of dinner table conversation.

Had he been trying to hurt her, or did it come effortlessly to him? Whatever the reason, it had made her all the more sure that she had been right in refusing his proposal.

But being right did not stop her from wanting him.

As she dipped her quill to start the next page the door swung open and Martin stepped into the room with her, greeting her with a look of surprise.

'I am here early,' she said, by way of an apology. 'But you had not come for several days and I thought...'

Of course, that made it clear that she had been lurking here every morning, hoping to find him.

He either did not notice or chose to ignore the truth.

'I have been attending my mother,' he said.

He did not look happy about it.

'You have my sympathies,' she replied.

'My apologies for her behaviour at dinner,' he said.

'I was warned that she could be difficult,' Felicity admitted.

'She was on rare form that night.'

She nodded.

He stood silent for a moment, and then closed the door, which was still standing open behind him. 'It is good to see you again…' he began, then paused again.

'I was not sure you would think so after our last parting here,' she admitted.

'My offer stands,' he said, looking her directly in the eye.

'As does my refusal,' she replied.

'I have missed you,' he said irritably. 'Even though it has only been a few days.'

'You will get over it in time, I am sure,' she said, with more confidence than she felt.

For her part, the loss of him felt as if someone had carved a piece from her heart and was now dangling it just out of reach.

'And suppose I do not *want* to recover from you?' he said.

But his expression was still annoyed rather than loving.

'We do not suit,' she said, trying to remind herself of the fact. 'You made that clear at dinner the other night. You think my plans for my future are a joke. Your mother doubly so.'

'They are not practical,' he said.

'And you think the sensible alternative is marrying into a family that views me with nothing but scorn,' she said, shaking her head. 'I am sure, if you wish to marry, there are better choices to be had than me.'

'I do not wish to be married,' he said.

'Nor do I.'

Certainly not to a man who could say that after offering, no matter how much she might love him.

'But that does not change the way I feel when I am with you,' he said, frowning.

Then he reached for her, as if a kiss would somehow erase what had just been said.

She pulled away and he looked at her in surprise.

'You are refusing me in this, too?'

'It is not possible to go back to the way things were. And since we cannot agree on a way forward, I think it wise that we do not continue.'

'At what point did you begin to use wisdom to decide your course of action?' he asked, his hands dropping to his sides.

'When you decided that you knew my future better than I did myself,' she replied. 'I do not wish to make love to you, and I certainly do not want to marry you. Since there is nothing more to say, I think it is best that you leave me in peace.'

She pointed to the door.

'You expect me to vacate my own space and cede it to you?'

'There are birds everywhere,' she said, waving her arms about her. 'But only one writing desk. Since my novel will be finished in just a few days, I am not issuing a lifelong ban.'

'Very well, then,' he said. 'Finish the damned book if that is all that matters to you.'

Then he turned and left, slamming the door so hard that the hide shook.

'You are back so soon?' his mother said, staring at him as he stormed into the drawing room where she sat. 'Were the birds uncooperative?'

'Very,' he said, trying to moderate his temper.

What he wanted to do…needed to do…was to go to the portrait gallery to talk with someone who understood him.

The fact that the 'someone' was an inanimate object would only convince his mother that he was fit for the madhouse and not a seat in the House of Lords.

'Perhaps you could try another location?' his mother suggested. 'There are birds everywhere.'

'So everyone keeps reminding me,' he snapped.

'Or you might visit Ophelia and help her with the plans for the upcoming ball,' she said. 'She has informed me that she does not need my help, but I suspect she is simply trying to avoid my company.'

'I wonder why,' he said, giving her a sour look.

'Of course, there is that Morgan girl in the dower house as well,' she said, then paused to observe him, as if waiting for a reaction.

He schooled his face into a neutral mask. 'She is no concern of mine.'

At least not any more.

'She is totally inappropriate,' his mother reminded him.

'For what?'

'For you,' she said—as if he had not realised that fact at their first meeting. 'No family to speak of…'

'Since I am not marrying her, that is not my concern either,' he said, a little too quickly.

'And the writing,' she said, with a *tsk* and a shake of her head. 'Someone will have to put a stop to that.'

'Someone other than me,' he replied.

As if you could—even if you wanted to.

'And her manners,' she added with a frown. 'She is far too outspoken.'

'Only because you could not cow her into silence,' he finished.

Emma had lived in terror of his mother, tying herself in knots by attempting and failing to please her. But it had been clear at dinner that Felicity had recognised a hopeless cause when she saw it and therefore had not bothered.

He could not help it. He smiled.

'You are not listening to anything that I am saying,' his mother said with a grimace.

'On the contrary. I heard every word. I just do not understand what it has to do with me,' he said. 'I have told you often enough that I have no intention of marrying. Why are you bothering to warn me away from Miss Morgan?'

Especially since she turned you down.

If his inner monologue was any indication, talking to his mother was almost as good as talking to the painting. Probably because, no matter what he said to her, she would not change.

'I am simply reminding you of your obligations,' she said with a firm smile. 'When you choose, you must choose wisely.

'Why is everyone suddenly doubting my common sense?'

'Everyone?' she repeated.

'It is as if you do not trust me to know what is best,' he continued. 'The next time I make an offer it will be to someone who does not refuse.'

'The next time?'

'It will not be to a girl who thinks only of her own happiness.'

'Of course,' his mother said, staring at him as if waiting for another outburst.

There would be none. He had said too much already.

He backed towards the door. 'And now I am going to my study. I do not wish to be disturbed until supper.'

'As you wish,' his mother said with a smug smile, and watched as he turned and left.

Chapter Sixteen

The day of the blasted ball had arrived.

He had been unable to think of it without adding that adjective since his last meeting with Felicity, almost two weeks ago. He did not wish to see her again, and had made it a point to be absent on those days when his mother had invited her and Ophelia to tea in order to plan the event, going to his hide in the only times he'd been sure it would be empty.

But even while he'd tried to watch his birds in solitude he had been conscious of the stack of paper behind him on the table, covered with an oilcloth to keep it safe from the dripping of the leaky roof.

He'd wanted to look at it, to see if there was any indication that she had reached the end. When she'd finished, she would leave.

For some reason that thought had made him more uneasy, rather than less. What if she left before he could speak to her one last time? He had no idea what he wanted to say, but there seemed to be something unexpressed nagging at the back of his mind.

Then he'd remembered that she had begun her book in his library, and hidden the first chapters behind some of the books. She would have to come back for them if she wanted to complete her work.

To make sure she would not be able to collect those pages without speaking with him he'd taken them hostage, locking them in his desk. If she wanted them she would have to come to him—which he would much prefer to his going to her. It would give him one last chance to change her mind—about either his offer or their affair.

But she'd made no effort to contact him, in person or in writing, and nor had there been any evidence that she'd searched the library for the missing pages. Perhaps she was waiting for tonight, when the house would be full of people...

By seven he was properly washed, shaved and combed, and dressed in an evening suit that he had not worn since before Emma had died. The formality of it felt strange—especially as he knew that he was going no farther than his own ballroom.

His mother was waiting at the foot of the stairs and she inspected him through her quizzing glass, spending an inordinate amount of time staring at his cravat before declaring the knot to be simplistic, but satisfactory for entertaining country gentry.

'And I suppose you have invited some of the girls on your list,' he said, giving her an equally critical look.

'Do not be ridiculous,' she said. 'None of them would bestir themselves from town at this time of year. This little gathering will be nothing more than a prelude for your return to London society, where you will meet them all.'

'I would not hold my breath,' he said, turning as the front door opened and Ophelia and Felicity entered the hall.

If possible, Felicity was even more beautiful than he remembered. She was wearing a white ball gown shimmering with crystal beads, and the fabric clung to her curves like a whispered sin.

'Miss Morgan,' he said, trying not to stare.

'Lord Woodley,' she replied with a curtsey.

'Step aside and let your aunt into the house, Martin,' his mother said, giving him a sharp poke in the ribs. 'Take us to the ballroom, so we may speak to the musicians before the guests arrive.'

As they walked to the ballroom Felicity stared around her at the candles, the flowers and the elegant buffet table, trying to look at anything but

Martin. He was resplendent in black, his shirt gleaming white against the wool of his coat, his dark hair combed smooth, with none of the unruly curl it had on those days when he went to watch the birds.

It had been almost two weeks since she'd seen him, and to be so near and pretend no interest was a special sort of torture. But it was one she'd brought upon herself in her decision to end what they'd shared.

She'd regretted it each day since, though she was still sure it was for the best. They could not go on as they had been doing, under his mother's nose, and nor could she accept an offer that had been given out of nothing more than duty.

But that did not make this night any easier. Tonight she was his honoured guest, and she would be the centre of attention for an entire room full of strangers.

She feared the moment she looked at him everyone would know what they had done together. She should have known better than to start an affair she did not know how to finish.

'Are you nervous?' whispered Lady Ophelia at her side.

'Very,' she said.

'Do not worry. The people here are friendly, and

as eager for a pleasant and successful evening as you are.'

'If your parents had given you an adequate come-out this would not intimidate you so,' the Duchess said, giving her a look that disproved Ophelia's encouragement. Then she held out a hand and said, 'Give me your dance card. Ophelia and I will make sure that the musicians know the order of play.' She gave Felicity another scathing look. 'And you, girl, must remain near the door, so that the guests can get a good look at you. Though in that dress they are not likely to miss you.'

'Then I am glad I chose it,' Felicity replied, refusing to let herself be bullied. 'I would not want to be overlooked at my own ball.'

The Duchess *hmph*ed in response, then went off to badger the master of the orchestra.

'I suppose I must go and protect the musicians,' Martin said with a sigh.

But before he left he turned to her and offered a brief smile of approval. The expression lasted only a moment and then it was gone, as was he, leaving her alone with Ophelia.

And now the first guests were arriving, their names being announced at the door by a footman so she need not be totally ignorant of their identities as they came into the ballroom, looking about them with smiles of approval.

Felicity noticed almost immediately that the Duchess had been right about the dress she had chosen. Though in London she had been a perennial wallflower, her mother had refused to allow her to be seen in anything less than the first stare of fashion. But many of the people they'd invited tonight had no reason to go to town for the Season, and were wearing styles that were several years out of date and not nearly as ornate as her embellished gauze gown.

Her *faux pas* did not seem to bother them. Though she might have been scorned in London for such a mistake, the young ladies here were excited to meet her and quiz her on the latest fashions. The gentlemen complimented her beauty, and seemed to be treating her as a nine days' wonder.

She responded awkwardly, unused to such sudden popularity, and was surprised to see her dance card nearly full before the music had even begun. She scanned down the list and regretted that there was no waltz. Though she had never danced it before, she had hoped that tonight might be her first chance to do so.

And if she had imagined dancing it with a certain marquess then it was better that no one knew the fact.

She would only call attention to herself by seeking him out to take the blank spot on her card. He would surely dance the first dance with her, at least. He was the host and she his honoured guest.

But when the time came he offered his arm to his mother, and left her to a baron from the next county, who trod on her toes. She smiled her way through the dance, then allowed herself to be led away by her next partner—a young farmer who was a much better dancer.

As the night progressed it seemed she stood up with every eligible male in the room. Everyone except her host, who had been avoiding the ballroom in favour of cards and wore black as if he was still in mourning.

Was it easier for him to allow people to think he still grieved than to admit that there might be room in his life for another?

When there was a break in the dancing she slipped from the ballroom, wandering down an unlit corridor towards the part of the house she was most familiar with: the library. The first half of her book still waited there, to be joined with its nearly completed ending.

She could not take it with her tonight. It was far too large to smuggle from the house. But it would be comforting just to visit it, and to sit in a quiet, dark room for a while. Though she was doing her best to enjoy the festivities, the crowd at the ball made her nervous.

But when she moved the books on the shelf where she'd left it aside, the niche she'd created was empty.

'Looking for something?'

Martin's voice came from the darkest corner of the barely lit room, startling her.

She spun to face him, peering into the gloom. 'What have you done with it?'

'Simply moved it from a common room, so that it would not be discovered before you were ready to collect it.'

'But you have not read it?' she said, half hoping that he had.

'I have not touched it other than to lock it in my desk,' he said, then added, 'If you want it back you will have to pay a forfeit.'

'Of what kind?' she asked, thinking of the burned first draft. Surely he would not be so cruel?

'Once, you gave me a kiss for a single sheet of paper,' he reminded her. 'Half a manuscript should be worth considerably more.'

'A strange request from a man who will not even look at me tonight, much less dance with me as other men have.'

He stood and walked towards her, circling her as

she turned. 'I did not trust myself to touch you.' He took her hand and pressed it against his, palm to palm. 'Not with all those people watching.'

He circled her again. Stepped away. Stepped in. Circled. And she followed him, step for step, as if she'd waited a lifetime for this silent dance.

'You feel what we are together? How right it is? How we move as one?' he said. 'I cannot hide that.'

'Nor can I,' she whispered.

He stopped, his fingers twining with hers, pulling her close as his other hand slipped about her waist. And then he was holding her, kissing her, slowly, gently, thoroughly.

He pulled away and went back to the chair he'd been occupying when she'd entered.

'Tomorrow, at eleven, I will bring the pages you were looking for to the hide and reunite them with their fellows. Whether you are there to thank me for the act is totally up to you.'

Chapter Seventeen

The next day Martin went to the hide just after breakfast, taking the manuscript pages with him, as promised. He was earlier than usual, and told himself that it was simply a desire to get away from his mother that had driven him from the house. But he knew that was a lie. The Duchess was sleeping late, after the excitement of the ball, and would not be up until luncheon.

The truth was, he wanted to see Felicity. More importantly, he wanted to be with her—in any way she would allow it. He was obsessed with the woman. Just as she was obsessed with her writing. Perhaps it was the secrecy of their affair that made his mind run wild. He'd known men to go mad over their mistresses and make fools of themselves. But such passion eventually burned itself out and they were themselves again.

That left him wondering where she was today. He

had not precisely told her that she must exchange her favours for the return of the manuscript pages. He'd leave them in any case. But maybe she had assumed as such and was insulted. It had been over two weeks since they'd last been together. Perhaps she was not missing him as he was her.

Then the door opened and she stepped into the room.

They stared at each other in silence for a moment, as if neither one wanted to look away. Then she glanced at the papers on the little table and paged through what he had brought, slipping them beneath the other stack of finished work.

She sighed in satisfaction and looked to him, smiling in relief. 'That had been playing on my mind. With your mother in residence, I could not exactly march into the house and get them for myself.'

'She wishes for you and Ophelia to come to dinner this evening,' he said, trying to be as casual as she was.

'I will relay the message,' she said.

'You had best not. We will not have been meant to see each other beforehand, so how would you know?'

She nodded. 'I had forgotten.'

They were silent again.

The pressure built between them, and he was about to speak when she blurted, 'I'm sorry.'

'For refusing my perfectly honourable proposal?' he replied, feeling the hurt rising again.

'The answer is still no,' she said. 'But I am sorry. I could have been kinder.'

'If this is some half-baked idea that you have got from Ophelia and her arrangement with the vicar...'

'It is not,' she said. 'It is just that I do not wish to settle for a man who can never love me. Is that so unreasonable?'

When put that way, it did not seem so. And she was probably right. If she ever wished to marry she would want what he'd had with Emma, not some pale imitation.

'Very well,' he said.

This was the moment when one of them should leave. *He* should leave. If they were not to be married, he should call a halt to what was going on between them.

Instead, he reached for her, and she stepped into his embrace.

'I have missed you,' she whispered.

The sound of her voice was all it took to make him hard. He'd thought that the heat of his desire for her would have burned away by now. But he wanted her even more than when she'd first touched him.

'We...'

'We shouldn't,' she finished for him. 'I know. But should and shouldn't doesn't matter to me any more. I want you.'

His hands shook as he undid the buttons on the back of her dress, pushing it down to her waist as she untucked his shirt and wrapped her arms around his ribs. Soon she was pushing him back towards the cot, laying him down in a tangle of half-shed clothes and straddling him, ready and willing to take him into her body.

He was happy to oblige. And now they were one, and he was lost in the feeling, in the shock of no longer being alone but a part of something better. She found his rhythm easily, as he had known she would, taking him deep and then almost parting from him, only to come back to him again. He was lost in the rightness of it...this claiming and being claimed, over and over, building to a pounding frenzy, with a fire of wanting in the blood and the brain.

The moment came when he should pull away and finish. But she was staring down into his eyes, into his soul, as if daring him to be brave enough to stay. To risk everything. To give everything. To take everything.

Perhaps that was what he had needed to do all along? If he crossed the final barrier and finished as he should, she could not refuse him again. Surely she would see that what they had done was irrevocable? Then they would have to be married.

She reached down between them, touching the place where they were joined as lightly as a blessing, a permission to do what he wanted. And then he felt her lose control, taking him with her in a thundering climax. It was good. So very good. And she was smiling like an angel who was staring into heaven.

How could this be wrong?

When they were done she kept him inside her, and he closed his eyes and felt himself drifting as she snuggled against him, her lips on his throat, her hands stroking his hair.

And then there was nothing but sleep...

He started awake, unsure if minutes or hours had passed. Probably the latter, judging by the way the sun was slanting through the windows of the hide.

It had been ages since he'd held a woman like this and been at peace. He knew there were things he had to say to her, and another proposal to make. But he did not want to break the silence. It was a sacred thing, and he would not be the one to ruin it. For a few more moments they could be halves of a whole, apart from the world.

When she finally pulled away from him it was

with a sigh of regret. They rose and dressed in silence, helping each other with shy smiles and gentle touches. And then he glanced out through the door, to make sure that they were as alone as he thought, and gestured her to precede him with a sweeping bow.

When she was gone he waited a half an hour before returning to his house, so there might be no risk that they were seen together, smiling like the lovers they were.

When Felicity arrived back at the house it was almost five, and Ophelia was clearly agitated.

'Where have you been?' she asked, frowning in disapproval.

'Reading under a tree,' she said, before realising that she carried no book with her.

If Ophelia noticed, she chose not to say.

'We are invited to the great house for supper and there is little time to get ready.'

'Of course,' she said, and then remembered that she should not know. 'I will go to my room and prepare,' she said, trying to appear penitent.

But she could feel the smile she had been wearing all afternoon playing at the corners of her lips, ready to break through like the sun from behind a cloud.

How was she going to sit at table with Martin and

keep their love a secret? For after this afternoon she was sure that was what they shared. He must know it too, even though he had not said anything. But she was sure he would propose again—perhaps even tonight.

She imagined him announcing in front of his mother that they were to be married, and that lady's look of horrified astonishment. He would ignore her protestations and say that there was no other woman for him, and they would share a secret smile as his mother collapsed in defeat.

Or perhaps he would pull her aside after the meal and get down on one knee, before taking her hand and making a proper declaration of his feelings. They would share a kiss before going back into the sitting room, hand in hand, to tell the Duchess and Ophelia.

Either would be fine with her. The particulars did not really matter so long as she saw the happiness in his eyes and heard the words of love he spoke. This time, when he proposed, she would say yes.

To prepare, she chose her favourite dress—the deep blue silk that suited Ophelia's borrowed pearls. She begged the maid to take extra care with her hair, and chose a style that left one saucy curl dangling at her left shoulder, like an invitation to mischief.

When she came down the stairs again Ophelia

nodded in approval, and they went out to the carriage that was ready to take them to the great house.

They arrived to find the Duchess waiting to greet them in the hall.

She gave Felicity her usual reproving look, then said, 'What is wrong with your hair?'

She touched it, searching for what might be out of place.

'You have lost a pin,' the Duchess insisted, staring at the curl. 'Go upstairs and have my maid set it right for you.'

'It is as I intended it,' Felicity replied with a firm smile.

'How odd.'

But the older woman shook her head and walked with them to the sitting room, where Martin was already waiting.

When she saw him her smile broadened, and she was surprised to realise how much she'd missed him, even though they had been together only hours ago.

'Miss Morgan,' he said, and bowed. 'Aunt Ophelia.'

Was there a warning in that simple greeting? A caution to be careful lest she reveal what they had done together?

Did she care? She wanted to sing it from the mountain tops, so that all would know the truth.

'Lord Woodley,' she replied, and could not help the way her curtsey made the curl bounce against her skin.

Beside him, his mother made a noise rather like a low growl.

'You must be hungry, Mother,' he said, giving her an oblivious smile. 'Come, let us go in to dinner.'

The meal passed in the usual way, with a string of veiled criticisms from the Duchess towards everything from the food to the current political climate. She deemed the lobster too rich, the sauce too buttery, and Wellington an idiot for allowing Napoleon to escape Elba.

It was a kind of relief. If the woman did not like butter, how could she possibly like Felicity?

The meal ended with no sign of a proposal and a raspberry iced cream mould that the Duchess called, 'too cold'. Then they retired to the sitting room for the evening and set up the card table.

Though Felicity would have much preferred Martin as a partner, she was relieved when he took on the job of handling his mother, taking the brunt of her complaints the few times when play did not go her way.

The night seemed interminable—probably because she was wishing that even a moment of it could be spent alone with Martin.

Perhaps, if she gave him an opportunity, he would seek her out as she'd imagined…

So she mentioned that she wished to find a book to take back to the dower house, and excused herself to go to the library.

Once there, she glanced at the connecting door, which was open. The study was lit, and his latest painting sat drying on a table near the window. She could not resist taking a peep, for his work was most impressive for a man who had not trained as an artist.

She stared at the little olive-green birds he had drawn, admiring the delicate shading of the feathers and wondering how much longer it would take him to finish his work.

It made her happy that they were both working on books. The subject matter of their two works could not be more different, but a writer was a writer, driven by the same spirit. That passion was something that would bind them together. They understood each other.

She went to his portfolio next, to take a look at the rest of the paintings. When she opened it she saw there was another pair of greenfinches, posed in almost the same way as those in the painting on the table. And beneath that, another.

She carefully paged down through the stack and

saw that he had done the same with owls and buntings and every other bird. He had made several studies and multiple paintings of the same species. She had to admire his thoroughness, but it seemed rather obsessive to her.

Had he done the same with the whole manuscript? The book had to be here, for she knew he did not leave it in the primitive place he'd made for himself in the woods. He must come back to the house to compile his notes.

And here it was, in a series of boxes behind the desk labelled volumes one to ten. She pulled the lid off the last box and found a stack of bound notebooks that was nearly ten inches thick.

How long was this book supposed to be?

She paged through the first notebook, which was neatly written, clear and complete, its subjects arranged alphabetically.

She turned to the last box and looked through it to find the last notebook, full of widgeons and yellow wagtails.

She struggled for a moment to think of any bird that might come after. Perhaps there was something missing from the middle? But when she checked through the other boxes the accounting of species seemed complete. The notebooks contained all the common sorts, as well as birds that she had never seen before. There was enough information here to make a respectable scholarly work.

When Martin found her she was sitting on the floor, surrounded by uncovered boxes and open notebooks.

'What are you doing in my study—again?'

He stood in the doorway to the library, staring at her with annoyance.

'Reading your book,' she said, spreading her arms to encompass the chaos she'd made of his orderly arrangement.

'I did not give you permission to look at my work,' he said, his eyes narrowing.

'After what we shared today, that is all you have to say to me?' she asked, still half expecting him to pull her to her feet and tell her what she wanted to hear.

His expression did not change. 'Do not confuse what we did with an invitation to reorder my life to suit yourself.'

He was speaking of the book. But there was a note in his voice that hinted at something great and untouchable that was still standing between them. Something that she'd hoped had been put to rest.

'Then what did it mean to you?' she said, almost afraid to ask.

'The same as it meant the last time we were to-gether,' he said. 'That we should be married.'

She stared at him in amazement. 'That is all?'

Had she really been so foolish as to give him all her love only to receive another empty offer in return?

Apparently she had, for now he was staring at her with a puzzled expression, as if he had no idea what she expected to hear from him.

She stood up and stepped between the notebooks and the thick portfolio of sketches and paintings. 'How long have you been working on this?'

'Since about six months after my wife died,' he said.

His *wife*.

He said the word as if there could only ever be one woman who would bear that title. If she married him—as she'd thought she wanted to—she would be nothing more than a poor second.

She stared down at the paintings…another symbol of his empty life. 'And when was it finished?' she asked.

'It is not…' he began.

'You are painting the same birds over and over again,' she said, flipping open the portfolio and spreading the plates.

'It is not right yet,' he said, stepping forward and taking a sketch out of her hand, before putting it carefully back into the portfolio and tying up the strings to close it.

'Have you seen all the species that the area has to offer?' she asked.

'I am not sure...' he muttered.

'You have seen the passage of several seasons twice over,' she reminded him.

'Perhaps next year...' he began.

'Or perhaps not,' she said, kicking open the notebook at her feet. 'Perhaps you have decided that it will never be good enough. Because once it is done you will have to do something with it.'

'It is not ready,' he insisted.

'The book is complete,' she said. 'You are the one who is not ready.'

'What right have you to tell me such a thing?' he said, outraged. 'You barely know me.'

She froze, shocked. She had thought, after what had happened today, that they knew each as well as two people could. He had looked at her as if he could see into her soul, and she had done the same to him. But perhaps what she'd seen in him had been only what she'd wanted to see—like those proposals she'd made up out of her overactive imagination.

She stared at him now, as if for the first time.

He stared back, still angry.

'If you cannot move on in this, how will you move

forward in other areas of your life?' she asked gently, giving him one last chance. 'Prove to me that you can let go of the past.'

'I have nothing to prove to you, Miss Morgan,' he said, just as formal as he'd been at dinner. 'I was the one to make the offer, after all. You are the one who rejected me in favour of a liaison.'

'And because of that you are telling me that what happened today meant nothing more to you?' she said.

'I enjoyed it—as did you—and my offer of marriage stands. But I fail to see what that has to do with my past or my work.'

'Or mine,' she said, thinking of the nearly finished book at the hide, and the fact that she need not remain here once it was done.

'They are not really the same things,' he said with a smile. 'What I have done is a scholarly work. Yours is…'

'Just my future,' she replied, feeling the familiar frustration like a weight on her chest.

Since he'd given her paper, and a place to write, she'd thought he understood how important it was to her. But he was looking at her with something like pity.

'As my mother said, young ladies often go through

such phases. But that is my life's work you have scattered on the floor about your feet.'

'And yet you are not serious enough about it to publish or to show it to experts now that it is done,' she said.

'When it is done—' he began.

'It is finished,' she said, gesturing at the notebooks on the floor. 'I could recommend my publisher. I could write a letter to Mr Ransom. You could take it to London today, if you wished.'

'I am not going to London—now or ever.'

This was a shocking admission from a man whose very future revolved around his seat in Parliament.

'And if I choose to publish I will not need your recommendation.'

'*If?*' she said, seizing on that one little word which was yet another sign that he was not ready for love. Not ready for her.

'It is not time,' he insisted.

'It will never be time,' she said. 'You want to stay here for ever, with your painted birds and your painted wife. Stuck in this place just as she is.'

'You have no right to speak of Emma,' he said.

'I have more than enough right. Enough to tell you that you are using your loss as an excuse to avoid anything and anyone that might hurt you again. You have the nerve to say that my plans are just transient things, but you have no plans at all.'

'What is all this shouting about?'

The Duchess was standing in the doorway to the study, Lady Ophelia one step behind her.

'None of your affair,' Martin said, without turning to look at her.

'We were discussing your son's book,' Felicity said, smiling at the Duchess.

'And Miss Morgan's imminent departure,' Martin added.

'Perhaps it is time for you to leave,' Ophelia suggested.

'It is,' Felicity replied. 'Lord Woodley and I have nothing more to say to each other.'

And with that she fled the room, and went outside to wait in the carriage.

Chapter Eighteen

Martin awoke with a start, reaching automatically in the empty bed beside him for a woman who was not there.

It was a strange thing to do. For when Emma had been alive she'd slept on his left. But a week ago, when he'd dozed with Felicity on that little cot in the hide, he had lain on his right side, as he did now, with her snuggled in his arms.

Since then he'd felt that emptiness to his right each night as he dozed, and again each morning before he rose—as if those few hours when they'd napped had made a lifetime's impression on him.

It was foolish of him. She'd made it quite clear the last time she'd seen him that they could have no future together.

Perhaps, with time, his body would understand what his mind already did. She was gone and was not coming back. But did he truly understand?

Last night he had dreamed, which he rarely did, for he seldom slept deeply enough to do so. This had been one of those deceptively happy dreams, of the family he should have had. They always ended in a nightmare, and he would wake to the reality of cold loneliness in a darkened bedroom. Then he would lie awake for the rest of the night, brooding on what might have been.

In this dream he had been at the great house in Ashton, and the halls had been full of joyful laughter. He'd been able to hear the children but had not been able to find them. They'd been playing a game with him, and he had walked the corridors searching for them, eager to see their smiling faces when he discovered their hiding place.

But no matter how many rooms he'd searched they'd always seemed to be just ahead—around the next corner or up the stairs, their happiness just out of reach.

In his sleep, he'd girded himself for the inevitable disappointment of the dream's end. But then he'd turned a corner and felt the rush of warm bodies pelting into him, little arms reaching out to encircle him and pull him close. And there, just beyond the tumult of the children, had been his wife.

But not his Emma, as it usually was. It had been Felicity.

She'd smiled at him, holding her arms out as well. He'd stepped into them...

And then he'd jolted awake and patted the mattress, searching for the comfort he was sure she would offer him.

When had he begun to think of her in that way? It was foolish of him. Their affair had ended. She had left him alone, as he had been before, free to do just as he pleased.

And right now it pleased him to do nothing at all. He no longer went to his hide, for he knew she would be there. He did not paint, for there was no point in drawing the same birds over and over. And there would be no more entertaining, for he could not bear to see Ophelia and listen to her make excuses for the absence of Miss Morgan, who claimed to be feeling too ill to take dinner with them.

He had told his mother to go home to Norfolk, but of course, she hadn't listened to him.

He had not thought it possible for his days to be any emptier than they had been. But it was as if Felicity had ripped away all the illusions he'd built to hide behind, leaving him with nothing but dreams of a future he could not have without her.

There might have been some comfort in knowing that she shared his pain. But when she'd spoken of the future it had involved the sale of her next book and her ability to manage without him. Could that be true? Or was it just another fantasy? Surely people needed love to survive, or they'd end up as he was—alone and bitter, unable to move forward or back.

He did not bother with a shave or a fresh cravat—for what was the point of putting on airs when he knew the day to be as pointless as the rest of his life would be?

He went down to breakfast to find a note from Ophelia beside his plate.

The Morgans have come to take Felicity home.
If you have anything to say to them, or her, now
is the time.

But what did he have to say that she wanted to hear? It certainly seemed that she wanted nothing to do with him as he was.

Tell her you need her.

He had hinted at the fact on several occasions and it had not been enough.

He winced. If the best he could manage was a vague expression of need, no wonder she had turned down his offer. What woman could survive on such thin gruel as that? He needed to be honest—with her and himself. He needed her as he needed air. Without her he was suffocating on his own pride.

Tell her you love her.

The thought came to him like a lightning strike, sudden and terrifying. But what else could he call that last day they'd had together? It had been pure, and wonderful, and when she'd tried to get him to admit the fact he had denied his feelings.

He was in love with her and he had been too afraid to say the words. And yet the feeling had been there in each touch, each glance, each kiss. More importantly, it was still here with him even when she was not. He would happily spend the rest of his life with her if she would let him.

But she would not. Not unless he was willing to change.

Then change.

The suggestion terrified him—which was proof that she was right. He had been avoiding his life and his future. Until he could embrace those, he would not be worthy of her love.

He would go to her now and promise that things would be different. He would give her the money to publish her next book, since that seemed to be so important to her. And then he would present himself to her father as a worthy suitor. Surely the man would not refuse?

But there was something he had to do first. He sprinted out of the study and up the stairs to the portrait gallery, stopping before Emma with his hands behind his back, a sheepish smile on his face.

'What can I say?'

He looked up into her beautiful blue eyes, knowing that now his future would be different.

'We both knew this day would come. No, that is not true. I suspect you knew long before I did, for you were always a most pragmatic woman. Me? Well, I thought my heart had died with you. But perhaps not.'

He paused, waiting for an answer. Of course there was none. In all the times he had spoken to her, she'd never really spoken back. Though he'd kept her alive in his memory, he must admit to himself that she was gone.

'She is different from you,' he said. 'But it is not as if I could ever replace you. What I have found is a woman who reaches places in my heart that I had not yet found when we were together.'

And it was true. He could not imagine Emma sitting quietly in the hide with him any more than he could imagine Felicity chattering so much that she scared the birds.

While Emma sparkled, Felicity glowed.

And he was surprised to find he could love them both.

'I seek your permission to remarry,' he said to the

portrait, gazing at her knowing smile, frozen for ever in paint. 'And I know I would have it were you here to give it. I have been faithful, even beyond death, but that was not what we promised, was it? I had to let you go once, and now it seems I shall have to do so again.'

He reached for his handkerchief, allowing himself a tear. But only one. For he could see a life that he had never expected, with a woman who was a perpetual surprise.

'I will never forget what we had together,' he said. 'It was beautiful. I can only hope that my future will be the same.'

And as always, when he spoke to her, Emma's smile told him what he wanted to hear.

From the portrait gallery he hurried to his room and summoned his valet, calling for a shave, fresh linen and his finest day coat.

Then he set out to the dower house, ready to meet the Morgans and win the hand of the woman he loved.

The End

Felicity wrote the words in her finest script, then wiped the tears from her eyes and set the quill aside. She'd told herself that it was only the drama of the story making her weep. The ending was quite sentimental, after all, with Columbina rescued by the hero and the abbot vanquished.

But that did not explain the tears shed yesterday, or the day before, or this morning before she'd begun to write. Those were all the fault of Martin. She'd had such hopes for him, imagining him as a great man on his way to something even greater. But it seemed that in their time together she had seen all there would ever be.

In another man that might not have mattered. Someone who did not have the capacity to love or the curiosity to study...someone dull enough to be content with what life offered...would not disappoint her so.

But Martin was meant for more than the life he was currently living. The title he would inherit and the scholarly work he had done were things meant to be shared with the world. And yet he preferred to remain alone, unhappy and unfulfilled. He refused to share himself with others, and thus would never really open himself to her.

She sighed and stood up. There was no point in remaining now that the book was finished. It would be safe hidden here until she could find a way to mail it to Mr Ransom. Then, with the money it would earn her, she would be able to escape this place and start her new life as an independent woman.

But what had seemed like a great adventure when she'd first planned it now seemed unspeakably lonely and rather dangerous. And until she'd had her courses she could not be sure that she was not carrying Martin's child.

He knew that as well as she did. And yet he still could not bring himself to offer her his heart. Perhaps someday he would realise his mistake, but by then it would be too late for them. She would just have to live with the consolation that she had loved once and well. It was more than many people would ever have.

She sighed, and then wrapped the finished manuscript in oilcloth to keep it safe until she could find a way to send it to London. Then she went back to the dower house, ready to spend the rest of the afternoon with Lady Ophelia.

When she arrived, she was surprised to see a hired carriage waiting at the front door. Her hostess had not said she was expecting visitors, but Felicity welcomed the diversion, hoping it would pull her from the funk she was in.

But then she noticed that the footmen were loading her bags into the back of the carriage. Was Ophelia putting her out for some reason? Or, worse yet, had Martin ordered her banned from his property?

She went into the house and sought out her hostess—only to find Ophelia in the sitting room, taking tea with her parents.

Her mother set her cup aside and rose to take her hands, leaning forward to kiss her. 'Felicity, it has been so long.'

'A few weeks,' she said firmly, trying not to flinch at this unexpected affection.

'We have missed you,' she said with a fond smile.

But her father looked as stern as ever.

She looked from one to the other of them, searching for an explanation for this surprising visit. 'You were the ones who sent me away,' she said.

'Only for long enough to clear your head,' her mother said. 'You really were behaving in the most outrageous ways, darling.'

'And you assume that I have now changed?' she said, trying not to look as annoyed as she felt.

'We are sure you have,' her father said with a cold smile.

'I understand that congratulations are in order,' Lady Ophelia said, giving her a disappointed look. 'I am surprised that you did not mention it earlier, but I am most happy for you, my dear.'

'You are?' she replied, baffled. It was not as if any of the people in the room were aware of the finished book in the hide, and nor would they think it worthy of celebration.

'If we could speak to Felicity alone for a few minutes,' her father said in an imperious tone, as if he had the right to banish Ophelia from her own sitting room. 'And then we will be on our way.'

'Of course,' Ophelia said, then rose and abandoned her.

Felicity gazed after her, then turned to her father, bracing herself for whatever was to come.

'We have found you a husband,' her father said in a clipped tone that brooked no argument. 'He is a solicitor—which will have to do, since you made no effort to bag a gentleman on your come-out.'

'I do not want a husband,' she said, feeling strangely numb.

'I did not ask you what you wanted,' her father replied. 'I told you what you will get. The announcement is already in *The Times.*'

'But I have not even met the man,' she said, horrified.

'I will tell you all you need to know,' her father continued. 'Mr Smollett is just beginning his career. Since the profits from that blasted book of yours made for a decent dowry, we have been able to convince him of your suitability.'

'You gave him my money?' she said.

She had accepted that her savings were lost to

her, but had never imagined that they would go to a complete stranger.

'Ladies do not need money,' he said, giving her another stern look. 'If they have families to take care of them, as you do, they do not worry about such things.'

'And a good husband will solve any problems in the future,' her mother said with a tight smile. 'Mr Smollett will be just that for you.'

'No,' she said, unable to stop the word.

By the incredulous looks on her parents' faces she knew that it was not what they wanted to hear.

'I will not marry someone I haven't even met,' she said, in a more modulated tone.

'You will meet him when we get back to London,' her mother said with another smile.

'And then you will marry him. Because beggars can't be choosers,' her father said, in a firm, no-nonsense tone. 'You have wasted enough time with your awkwardness and your foot-dragging. This should have been settled three Seasons ago, when you were first out. Now you will take who we have found for you and be grateful.'

'I do not need a husband,' she said firmly. 'I am quite capable of supporting myself.'

'With your scribbling?' her father said with a

sneer. 'It is not healthy to live with your head in the clouds, girl.'

'My first book did quite well for itself,' she said firmly, trying not to think of the money they had stolen from her.

'And how likely is that to happen again?' her mother asked with a pitying shake of her head.

'The second book is already finished,' she blurted— then immediately regretted it.

'Bring it here and I will throw it on the fire— just as I did in London,' her father replied. 'I told you then that there will be no more nonsense and I meant it.'

'You cannot force me to do this,' she said, taking a step towards the door.

'I can,' he said, blocking her way. 'You are leaving with us today, whether you like it or not. From here you will go to London to be married or to the Stanhope Asylum, where you will stay until you have learned the folly of disobedience.'

'I am not mad,' she said, though by the look in her father's eyes she rather thought he was.

'Then stop behaving as if you are and accept the man we have found for you,' he said, grabbing her wrist as she tried to push past him and escape.

She struggled for only a moment—long enough to prove that if he meant to drag her from the room and force her into the carriage she was not strong enough to stop him.

Suddenly the plight of poor Columbina in her story was all too real. But this time there would be no gallant hero coming to the rescue. She had only a few coins in her purse and could not afford to strike out on her own.

She was all alone.

'We are doing what is best for you,' her mother said, in a voice clearly meant to calm them both. 'You will see that once you are married. Soon you will have children to think of, and all this foolishness will be forgotten.'

Foolishness. That was all her life's work was to them. And to Martin as well. Why did no one believe in her? And what were the odds that this Mr Smollett would be any different?

And what was she to do if she was with child? Wouldn't it be better to hide her mistake in a marriage of some kind instead of trying to manage on her own? She could summon Martin and beg him to take her back, but would he want her if she was already promised to another man, or would he view it as a narrow escape?

She could feel unshed tears at the back of her throat as she imagined his relief when he discovered that he did not need to marry her after all.

'What will it be, girl?' her father asked, releasing her wrist. 'Marriage or the madhouse?'

It was an untenable choice. But it would be far easier to escape from a marriage than it would from a locked cell.

Really, there was no choice at all.

'I will meet him,' she said, taking deep breaths to control her panic. 'But I will make no promises until then.'

'You will see,' her mother said, clapping her hands together as though the matter was settled. 'It is for the best.'

And then, before she could think more on the matter, they had said their farewells to Ophelia and were in the carriage and on the road.

Chapter Nineteen

'What do you mean, she is gone?' Martin stared at his aunt, unable to believe what she had just said.

'They were back on the road little more than an hour after they'd arrived,' she said, wringing her hands. 'I tried to delay them, so you might at least say goodbye. But Mr Morgan was very eager to get Felicity back to London so she might meet her betrothed.'

'She has a fiancé? She did not mention any such thing to me.'

'Nor to me,' Ophelia replied. She reached for the copy of *The Times* that was sitting on the table beside them. 'But it must have been a plan some time in the making, for it has already been announced in the papers. Mr Morgan brought this along with them when they arrived.'

'This has to be a mistake,' said Martin, staring at the date on the paper. 'She was here when the announcement appeared. How could she have agreed to it?'

'Perhaps she is less than enthusiastic about the union,' Ophelia said with a shake of her head. 'Women without means are often forced by their parents to accept such decisions.'

'She has means,' he insisted. 'Or at least she claims she does.' But then, she had also claimed she would never marry. 'She has written another book,' he said, grasping at the last remaining straw. Although how much that would amount to he had no idea.

'Well, she did not have it with her when she left for London. If she had, her father would most certainly have taken it from her and destroyed it. After their embarrassment over the first book they intend to be most careful that she does not repeat her previous behaviour.'

Which meant the manuscript was probably abandoned in the hide. What was he to do about that?

He offered a silent curse.

And there was another question, which pained him more than the matter of her book. If she was going to marry anyway, why had she been so against marrying *him*?

He turned back to Ophelia. 'What did she say about this fellow?' He glanced at the paper. 'Edwin

Smollett? Has she ever spoken of him to you? How did she seem when her parents talked to her?'

'I have no idea. They spoke to her alone in the parlour, and when they exited it appeared that the matter had been settled.'

'Did she leave any message for me?' he asked, not sure whether to hope or despair.

'She said I was to say goodbye to you,' Ophelia said, obviously just as disappointed as he that there was not more to share.

Had everything she'd told him been a lie?

He refused to believe it.

'They are forcing her to do this somehow. She does not want to be married,' he said firmly.

'I do not blame her,' Ophelia replied. 'But her parents have plans for her and have left her little choice in the matter.'

That was probably the truth. The question was, what was he to do about it?

'If she'd accepted my offer they'd have no hold over her.'

And if he'd offered properly they'd be halfway to Scotland by now and planning their future.

'You offered for her?' Ophelia started in surprise. 'You have said nothing about that.'

'Because she refused me,' he said, embarrassed

to admit it. 'I was coming here to appeal to her parents on the matter and offer again.'

'Perhaps she refused because she already knew of this Mr Smollett,' Ophelia said, tapping the paper. 'If so, she is a most duplicitous young lady and I did not know her as well as I thought.'

'She did not lie,' he said. 'I am sure of it.'

If he could do nothing else, he could trust that she had been honest with him. If he loved her, he owed her that.

He stared down at the paper in his hand, then tossed it aside. 'If she does not want this marriage then I will find a way to free her.'

And then he would put his offer to her again.

When he returned to his home his mother was, as usual, more ready to rub salt into his wounds than to offer balm.

'We are all lucky to be rid of her,' she said with a nod. 'She had a most fractious disposition.'

'You are speaking of the woman I love,' he said, smiling. After so many weeks of denial, it felt good to say the words out loud. 'I mean to marry her if she'll have me.'

'She will have you,' his mother said. 'She is a fool else.'

'And you disapprove, I suppose?' he said, waiting for the diatribe he was sure would follow.

'It is not my place to approve or disapprove of the women you marry,' she said, with a wave of her hand meant to dismiss all her previous behaviour. 'I most definitely do not approve of you moping about in the country with no direction. If you admit that you wish to marry someone, it is a step in the right direction.'

'There are complications,' he admitted. 'She swore she did not want to be married—to me or anyone else.'

'And yet she is now engaged,' his mother reminded him. 'Young ladies today do not know their own minds.'

'Felicity is well aware of what she wants,' he said. 'She does not want to be married. She has insisted from the first that her writing is more important than any offer she might get.'

His mother nodded. 'Like you and your birds.'

'And yet even though she claimed it was so important to her she did not bother to take the book with her when she left,' he said, pondering on the stack of paper he had brought in from the hide. 'It appears to be finished, and yet she did not take it to the publisher.'

'Also like you and your birds,' his mother said.

He winced. 'We are not talking about me. She is totally different from me.'

For one thing, she had been supportive of *his* work. In response, he had been nothing but dismissive of hers.

'If she has left this here it is because her father forced her to leave in a hurry and against her will,' he said.

'How gothic,' his mother replied. 'It is like something from *The Mad Monk of Montenero*.'

'You know about *The Mad Monk*?' he asked, surprised.

'As would you, if you lived in London—where you should be,' his mother said with a frustrated huff. 'It is the most popular book of the Season. Everyone is dying to know the identity of the author and when they can get their hands on the sequel.'

'But that is Felicity's book,' he said, feeling a strange rush of pride.

'Miss Morgan?'

'The girl you took such pleasure in berating,' he said, his smile turning smug.

'I have had dinner with the author of *The Mad Monk*?' his mother said, stunned.

'Her parents were embarrassed by the book and sent her here to keep her from writing more,' he replied.

'But they are doing her no service in denying her the money and acclaim that will come with the revelation that she is the author,' she said, shaking her head in disbelief.

He was stunned too. 'She told me that she could survive very well on the money earned from her writing,' he said.

And he had refused to take her seriously.

'She may have no family to speak of,' his mother said with a disapproving sniff, 'but she will have a tidy little fortune of her own once the receipts are totalled. And if there is another book...'

She eyed the manuscript on the table with an avarice Martin had never seen in her before.

'Do you want to read it?' he asked.

Her impression changed to one of eagerness. 'Would she mind?'

He was not sure. She had refused him once, but she had not finished it then, and nor had he been one of her eager readers.

'I think it will be all right. Since you will be related to her if I can find her and persuade her to accept my suit.'

His mother was still eyeing the book as if she could not believe her good fortune. 'I might quite like having an author in the family...'

'As the future Duchess?' he said, surprised to have anything like her approval.

She shrugged. 'If she takes it into her head to be your marchioness, I do not think my objections will stop her.'

'That is probably true,' he said, thinking of how she had reacted to his mother's criticisms thus far. 'But neither of us will have to worry about it if I cannot find her and persuade her to marry me. The least I can do while readying to meet her is to read her work.'

To that end, he went to the study and penned a discreet note to the bookshop in Telford, stating that he wished to purchase a copy of *The Mad Monk of Montenero*, and adding with some embarrassment that it was for his aunt.

The footman he sent returned with a neatly bound package, accompanied by a letter stating that they had been able to procure the last set they had of the first printing, and that the five-volume collection was very popular with aunts all across the country.

There was a decidedly cheeky tone to the note, Martin thought. As if the bookseller questioned the existence of his aunt. He resisted the urge to write back and tell him that the woman lived just up the road from him, and he meant to give it to her as soon as he was finished with it himself.

He probably would not read the entire thing. He just meant to give it a quick skim and then head to London in the morning. Perhaps he'd read the first volume if it held his interest...

When the footman came to call him to supper, he realised he had forgotten to dress for dinner—which was hardly uncommon. He went to the table as he was. He took the book with him, prepared to be upbraided by his mother for his rudeness. But she was dining in her room with the manuscript from the hide and could not be bothered to join him.

He took volume two and a glass of port to the sitting room after dinner and continued to read.

His drink remained untouched.

He carried it to bed as well.

The next day it rained, which made for an awful day to travel and an excellent day for reading. In any case, he was too tired to go out, having been up late the night before with volume three.

When he closed the cover on the final volume it was nearly supper time again. He eyed volume one with curiosity, wondering if a reread might be in order.

The material was as salacious as *The Times* had said. It was not the sort of thing a young lady should be reading, much less writing. That scene in the dungeon of the abbey, for example...

Did abbeys have dungeons? He rather doubted it. But neither did they have tiger pits. Nor were there fjords in Florence. Felicity knew as much about Italy as he did ladies' millinery. Further research might render a sequel more accurate. Perhaps a honeymoon in Italy was in order.

But while he had been reading it had not seemed to matter at all. The book was readable to the point of being addictive, and he had to admit a perverse curiosity as to what the twin sister Columbina would do to escape the abbot.

He had to tell Felicity, and find out what she was going to write next. And he had to put a stop to this nonsense with Smollett and marriage to anyone but him.

But first he went to his mother's room to get the sequel.

Chapter Twenty

Felicity remembered London as being nicer than it was.

When she had travelled to Shropshire she had dreaded the time to be spent in the country, away from the bustle of the city. But actually it had seemed easier to write there, since there had been minimal supervision and a relationship more passionate than she'd imagined possible.

At the thought of Martin, her heart clenched. If she was honest, the country wasn't the thing she missed.

What was she to do without him?

Get married, apparently.

Since they'd come home she'd not been allowed out of the house without a chaperon—as if her father feared she would run away given the chance. But, since he had not reinstated her allowance, she lacked the money to get any distance from home.

And now that she had met her husband-to-be she was almost too despondent to flee.

She looked across the sitting room at Mr Edwin Smollett and tried not to contemplate her future. He was just the sort of man she'd expected her father to choose for her—a self-absorbed social climber who had not stopped talking about himself and his business since the moment he'd sat down to tea. He was a solicitor who claimed to handle the estates of his clients with discretion, though how it was possible for him to do so while bragging of his connections with them she was not sure.

'And then there was the will of Lord Ernest Battingly, who was second cousin to the Earl of Marshlake.' He paused, waiting for her response.

'The second cousin? How interesting,' she said, and then let her mind wander until the next response was required.

What would he say if she told him that she'd dined with a duchess just a few days ago, and that he could take the Earl's second cousin and dump him in the Thames, for all she cared.

Then she remembered her father's threats of a more drastic cure for her rebellion and remained silent.

His monologue continued, and the smile froze on her face as she imagined a lifetime of such talk. Or perhaps he would be too busy with his important clients to talk to her at all.

That would be an improvement.

If he was busy at work she might have time to write. It would be the third time she'd had to start her second book. And really, copying out the story one more time would not be that hard, since she knew the words quite by heart.

But at the moment the idea of writing seemed both dangerous and painful, since it reminded her of the time she'd spent with Martin. She had not been able to say a proper goodbye to him when she'd left, and she wondered if that had angered him, or if he had been too immersed in his bird studies to care. Worse yet, he might be relieved that she had gone away. He had been quite angry with her the last time they'd been together, and she with him as well.

But there was nothing about that conversation that she wished to apologise for. It was one thing to grieve for a lost love—quite another to use that loss as an excuse to retreat from life. She would not go so far as to call Martin a coward, but it was clear he was not the hero she'd imagined him to be.

It was probably better that the break between them had been both quick and clean.

Mr Smollett had paused again, and this time her mother was the one to reply.

'And the Baron recommended you to his acquaintance? Isn't that impressive, Felicity?'

The question hit her like an elbow in the ribs and she dragged her mind back to the conversation. 'Very much so,' she said, wondering what it was that she was agreeing to.

'But I am talking far too much,' Mr Smollett said, as if sensing her waning interest. 'I have not even come to the reason for my visit.'

'And what is that, sir?' she asked, trying to look interested.

'I have brought you a gift.'

'You are too kind,' she replied, hoping it was not a betrothal ring. She did not want to wear a sign of his ownership a second sooner than was necessary.

'I took the liberty of telling the maid to bring it when I rang,' he said, going to the bellpull and summoning a servant as if he were in his own home.

A few moments passed and then the door opened and the maid struggled in with a large object swathed in a red velvet cover. She set it down on a side table and Mr Smollett stepped forward to pull the gold tassel that held the cloth in place.

'For you, my dear,' he said, and stepped aside to reveal a startled canary.

At this sudden exposure the poor thing took off

from its perch and flapped pitifully at the bars of its cage, desperate for escape.

'It's…' She was unable to complete the sentence, for the only word that came to mind was *horrible*.

When she did not say anything more, her mother answered for her. 'How thoughtful of you to remember.' She gave Felicity a pointed look. 'I told Mr Smollett that while you were in Shropshire you had taken up birdwatching. He has got this especially for you.'

'Thank you,' she said automatically, wondering if it was more cruel to keep the bird confined, or to release it in the park where it might be eaten by a hawk.

'What will you name it, Miss Morgan?' Smollett asked, oblivious to her disgust.

She stared at the panicked bird and said the first thing that came to mind. 'Persephone.' For wasn't the little thing consigned to a sort of hell?

'A beautiful name—as is her owner,' he said, apparently unaware of the context. 'And now I must go. My business will not wait. But I will visit again soon. And, of course, we will see each other at our engagement ball next week.'

'Of course,' she said, trying not to think of their first public appearance as a couple.

'Good day, then,' he said, looking at her expectantly.

Was he waiting for some physical sign of gratitude? A kiss on the cheek, perhaps? Or at least a hand-clasp. If so, he could go to the devil. But how was she ever to manage as his wife when she could not bring herself to touch him?

'Good day,' she said, not turning from the cage.

When he had gone, her mother asked, 'Are you all right?' coming to her side and giving her a nudge.

She was not. But there was no point in telling her mother, who had no power to change things even if she wanted to. So she took a deep breath, willed herself to be strong, forced a nod and changed the subject.

'Why did you think I had taken up birdwatching?'

'That was what Lady Ophelia said you were doing when we arrived in Shropshire,' she said.

'I see.' She twined her fingers in the bars of the cage, wondering for a moment which side of them she was on.

'Perhaps later you can write to her and thank her for the visit…tell her that all is well with you,' she prompted.

'Of course,' Felicity said with a sigh.

'And then we must write a few more invitations to the ball,' she added in an encouraging tone.

'I thought we had finished,' Felicity said, surprised.

'For the most part,' her mother said, in a wheedling tone. 'But there is one more in particular that I wish you to send. The scandal sheets say that the Marquess of Woodley has returned to London for the remainder of the Season.'

Felicity felt her throat close at this announcement, unsure of what she could say in response.

'He is Lady Ophelia's nephew and the heir to Ashton. You must have met him while you were away. His house is very near to hers,' her mother said, and then stared at her for confirmation.

'I did,' Felicity said. Then, when more seemed to be expected, she added, 'He was a most interesting gentleman.'

'And so sad,' her mother said. 'He was quite the wag a few years ago. The toast of London. His wedding was the talk of the Season and broke many hearts.'

'Including his own,' Felicity added. 'He swore he would never marry again after his wife's death.'

'Well, time has changed his mind,' her mother said triumphantly.

'More likely his mother has,' Felicity said. 'She was visiting when I left.'

'The Duchess of Ashton was in Shropshire?' her mother said, amazed.

'I saw her on several occasions,' Felicity said with a nod.

'And you did not speak of it?' her mother asked, shocked. 'Tell me all. What was she wearing? What of her jewellery? Her hair? Tell me everything.'

'It was all quite ordinary,' Felicity replied, wishing the conversation could get back to Martin and his change of heart. When they'd argued he had been quite adamant that he would never come to London. What had possessed him?

'But you met a *duchess*,' her mother corrected, leaning forward as if to catch every word.

Felicity sighed and related details of each interaction she could remember, including the Duchess's opinions of her behaviour, which made her mother wring her hands in dismay.

'I have warned you often enough that your behaviour will do you no service in proper society. Let this be a lesson to you,' she said.

'It is too late in any case,' Felicity replied. 'I was who I was when I met the Marquess and his mother. And now...'

'Now, when you meet them again, you will be able to assure them that trouble is all behind you,' her mother said proudly.

'Meet them again?' Felicity said, silently praying that would never occur.

'You are about to have your engagement ball,' her mother replied. 'And since I now know that Woodley is a friend of the family...'

'Hardly,' Felicity replied.

She could not think of him as a friend, for they had been far more than that—and far less as well.

'It will do us no harm to invite him,' her mother said with a hungry grin. 'Now that you have met him, it would seem strange if we did not.'

'We certainly shall not,' Felicity said, appalled.

'I shall do it myself,' said her mother, clearly unwilling to miss the opportunity. 'It will give you an opportunity to introduce Mr Smollett to the Marquess.'

'Why would I want to do that?' she asked. 'What could they possibly have in common?'

The one thing she could think of was something no two gentlemen would ever want to discuss. An awkward meeting like this was something she had never thought of when she had been becoming a woman with a past.

Martin had insisted that he was never leaving his house. Why couldn't he have kept his promise?

'It might open up opportunities to your future husband,' her mother said, with a look of disgust at her ignorance. 'Perhaps Woodley is in need of a law-yer. Or maybe, based on his acquaintance with you, Woodley will be willing to sponsor Mr Smollett as a member of his club.' Now her mother looked enrap-tured at the bright future ahead. 'First the engage-ment and now a marquess... This Season is turning out to be better than ever I hoped.'

But in Felicity's opinion things seemed to be get-ting worse.

By the time Martin arrived in London he had completed his reading of Felicity's second book, which was every bit as satisfying as the first. The hero of the story was tall and dark—which was not unusual, he supposed. The story was set in Italy, where many gentlemen fitted that description. But when the fellow in the book stopped to tell his trou-bles to a passing bird, he suspected she had taken some inspiration from her time with him in the hide.

Martin could not decide whether to be flattered or embarrassed. Did she truly see him as such a para-gon? It certainly had not seemed so when they'd last talked. Of course, at the time he had belittled her and her work. Who could blame her for leaving him?

But he was now in a position to make it up to her. Even if she truly meant to marry someone else he would see to it that her work was published, just as she'd intended. Then perhaps she would believe him when he saw her again and told her how wrong he had been about everything.

After a brief stop at the Ashton townhouse, to change out of his travelling clothes, he called for the carriage to take him to Mr Ransom the publisher, on Paternoster Row.

That man greeted him with an owlish look and an equally suspicious glance at the valise he carried, which contained the manuscript. But all hesitation evaporated when he heard the Woodley title. Then he led Martin to a small office, where he was presented with tea and Ransom's full attention.

Once they were alone, Martin said, 'I have come as an agent for the young lady who wrote *The Mad Monk of Montenero.*'

Ransom's reaction was immediate. He leaned forward in excitement, and then sat back again, staring at Martin sceptically. 'How might you know that young lady, my lord?'

At this, Martin had to suppress a grin, for he did not want the man to think that their acquaintance was more intimate than any gentleman should admit.

'She is a friend of my aunt,' he said at last. That sounded harmless enough. 'If you doubt the truth, then I will tell you that I know she is Miss Felicity

Morgan. She has recently returned to London, and I suspect she is being prevented from visiting you.'

The publisher sighed in relief. 'I thought you might have been sent to tell me to stop publication, for I have taken the liberty of proceeding with a second printing without her permission. She disappeared in the middle of discussing it with me and I have heard nothing from her for several weeks.' The man leaned forward, obviously concerned. 'I feared something might have happened to her.'

'She is well, I assure you,' Martin said. 'But her parents are trying to prevent her from proceeding with her career.' He smiled, feeling quite like the gallant hero in her book. 'I have come to rescue her.'

'Do you have her written permission to do so?' the man asked, quashing his romantic fantasy.

'Not as such,' Martin hedged. 'But I am acting with her best interests at heart—much as you were by printing a second edition. Might I ask how you paid for such a thing? As she explained to me, there was a considerable initial outlay of funds for the first printing.'

'I took the money from the profits of the sale of the first edition. Even after giving her the first monies she received, I was left holding three hundred pounds with no way to get it to her.'

'Three hundred pounds?' Martin echoed, amazed

at how wrong he had been about her prospects. She had not been exaggerating when she'd said she would be able to live on her own. She still might if he could persuade her away from her parents and this supposed fiancé.

He set the valise on the desk. 'I have in my possession the manuscript of her next book. I have read it, and it is even better than its predecessor.'

Ransom's eyes grew as wide as if Martin had dropped a bag of pound notes on the desk, and that was probably how he saw this new work.

'And how did you come by this…? No, wait…do not tell me.' He smiled back, his greed overcoming all questions. 'We must assume she wishes it to be published, or she would not have written it.'

'It was left on my property, which I think means I can do as I wish with it,' Martin said to reassure him. 'In case I am wrong, I will provide the money for the printing. There will be no financial burden upon her.'

'Then there is no reason I cannot send it to be set today,' Ransom said, and then added, 'If that is all right with you, my lord?'

'That is most satisfactory,' Martin said. 'But there is one small change I wish to make.'

'Anything you wish, my lord,' Ransom said.

He made his request. And then they spent the rest of the afternoon securing Felicity Morgan's future.

Chapter Twenty-One

The night of the engagement ball arrived, and as her maid put the final pins into her hair Felicity stared at her reflection in the dressing table mirror, experimenting with expressions. She was supposed to be happy. She had best learn to look it.

But, try as she might, the same worried frown kept reappearing on her face. How was she going to convince her betrothed that she had any interest in him if she could do no better than this?

It occurred to her that it might not matter to him one way or the other. He had agreed to the marriage before he'd even met her, based on the size of her dowry. A dowry she had earned herself.

The frown appeared again, and she smoothed it away.

He wanted money. Nothing more than that. He had shown no interest in her feelings or opinions so far, and it was unlikely to change after they were wed.

'You look beautiful, miss,' the maid said, smiling at her in the mirror.

'Thank you,' she answered.

The maid was right. She looked her best. Except for the frown.

She rose and walked through the open bedroom door and down the stairs to where her fiancé and her parents waited to take her to the room they had hired for the festivities.

Mr Smollett was smiling up at her like a man admiring a newly acquired possession. 'Miss Morgan,' he said, bending low over her hand and letting his lips brush her knuckles.

She tried not to shudder and practised her smile. 'Sir.'

'I have hired a carriage to take us to the ball,' he said, leading her towards the door. 'But when we are married we will have to buy a brougham and matched pair.'

Keeping horses and an equipage in London was expensive. As she let him help her up into her seat she subtracted the cost of this future carriage from her earnings. Then she looked out of the window and lost herself in the beginnings of a story that she would probably never be allowed to write.

Once they arrived at their destination he led her into a room that was already filling with guests, leaving her at the door as he went to check on the orchestra and refreshments.

'He is so thoughtful,' her mother announced.

Her father grunted in agreement.

But Felicity watched as he snapped at the servants and complained about the wine, wondering how long it would take before she did something that disappointed him. It would probably not occur until after the knot was tied, for he would not want to jeopardise the windfall he expected.

But she had best not think of that now.

She forced a smile and greeted the next guests to arrive, accepting the congratulations of dozens of strangers and allowing Mr Smollett to lead her out for the first dance of the evening.

He moved gracelessly through the steps and she followed, equally stiff.

'Why can't those musicians keep an even tempo?' he said, glaring over his shoulder at their leader.

'It does not matter,' she said, trying to catch and hold his attention with her best false smile.

Then she imagined what it might have been like dancing with Martin, had they dared to do so, letting her mind wander, just as it always did.

Her mother had insisted they invite him this evening, but they had received no response. For the sake of her sanity, she hoped he had thrown the invitation away unopened.

After what seemed like for ever the dance was over and Mr Smollett offered her a curt bow, as if relieved that his obligation was done.

'If you need me I will be in the card room,' he said, and left her.

Felicity looked after him, wondering if this was his habit at all balls or just the ones he hosted. If he was an inveterate gambler it might explain his interest in her money.

There was a chance that once they were married she would be even more miserable than she was now. But for the moment she was free of him, and she could not help but smile in relief. Then, without meaning to, she let her eyes stray to the door, looking for the one guest she both dreaded and longed to see.

By half past nine she had given up, and she was trying to relax in her role as guest of honour when the doors to the room opened one last time and Martin appeared.

He paused as the footman announced him, smiling down at the crowd from the head of the short flight of steps that led to the main part of the room, then sauntered lazily into their midst as if the place belonged to him.

It was a confidence she had not seen in him at any

304 *A Scandalous Match for the Marquess*

time in Shropshire—even in his own home. He had exchanged the black clothing he'd worn to his last ball for a blue coat and white breeches that must have come fresh from the tailor.

This must be what her mother called 'town bronze'. She had heard the term but had never understood it before. Martin seemed to gleam with it. His smile, which she had seen so rarely in the country, was dazzling. Around her she could hear young ladies sighing and married ladies remarking that it was a shame it had taken him so long to return to what was clearly his element.

She should greet him. But she stood frozen on the opposite side of the room and watched, terrified. What was she to say to him? He had been so easy to talk to in the country. But everything was different now. *He* was different.

He made no effort to catch her eye, but went to her mother instead, bowing over her hand and making her blush like a schoolgirl as another partner came to collect Felicity for the cotillion. Martin would probably have to stand out, for most of the young ladies' dance cards were full.

But, no. He went to an isolated corner and prevailed upon a wallflower to stand up with him, treating her with the same courtesy he would have shown if she was the loveliest girl of the Season. He did the same for the next dance, and the next, escorting unpopular girls out onto the floor and leading them gracefully through the steps, smiling as they chattered at him, near to overcome with excitement.

It made Felicity wish that she was still the social failure she had been before going to the country. Then perhaps he would have come and found her, dancing with her and leaving a beautiful memory at their parting.

Of course she would not have thought him capable of such social grace when she'd first met him. While she had been a failure in London, he had been an obvious recluse. Their time together had changed them both. Now she was to be married and he had gone back to being the person he had been before tragedy had struck him down.

Perhaps it was vain of her, but she thought she deserved some credit for bringing him back to himself...

She had been about to think it love. But they had never used that word between them, and nor did she think they ever would.

Was it possible to bring this much change to a person with a thing he didn't know existed?

And why had he come to her now that it was too late?

If the man in the room with her now had offered

for her, this smiling sophisticate with the kind eyes and perfect manners, she'd have forgotten her vow not to marry and said yes in a heartbeat.

But when he had proposed he had still been adamant about a solitary future, and she had not wanted to be alone and unloved in her marriage. What a joke it was that she'd now said yes to exactly the sort of union she had once feared, only to have him come to London so she might watch him make nice with every other girl in the room.

When the dance ended he escorted his partner to her chair and got her a glass of punch, making polite conversation for a time before ceding her attention to the next gentleman who would dance with her.

Another gentleman came to retrieve Felicity, as well, and she dragged her attention away from the Marquess to show proper courtesy to her partner. But as they danced her mind remained fixed on Martin…on what he might be doing and who he might be doing it with.

Did he mean to ignore her all night? Was she to ignore him as well? Surely that would be more suspicious than greeting each other fondly.

But how fondly? They had not parted on the best of terms.

Now that they were apart she could not shake the desire to apologise to him, and to admit that everything she'd done since coming to London had been an enormous mistake.

But what concern of his was that? She had been quite clear, from beginning to end, that their relationship was a temporary thing that might not even last the duration of her stay in the country. She could not go to him now and insist that she had changed her mind.

Still, it felt like a slap in the face for him to come to her engagement ball and make her watch as he searched for a wife. She had invited him to do so, of course. But he needn't have done it.

The dance ended and her partner led her to the side of the room. She checked her dance card to see who was to partner her next. The upcoming dance was the waltz, and she had left it open, assuming her fiancé would come to claim it. But it appeared that he had no such notion, for she could not see him anywhere in the room.

She allowed herself an impatient sigh—then looked up to find Martin approaching. He was wearing the same smile he had given to the wallflowers, and he bowed deeply over her hand.

'Miss Morgan…so nice to see you again.'

'My lord,' she said, curtseying. 'So kind of you to grace us with your presence.'

'And your future husband?' he said, looking around the room. 'Where is he?'

'In the card room, I believe, my lord,' she said, forcing a smile to tell him that she was not concerned by the fact.

'Well, you must not stand idle for the waltz,' he said, offering her his arm.

'I do not want to monopolise your time if there is someone you would rather dance with,' she said, desperate to evade him.

'Felicity,' he said, in a low tone that danced along her nerves. 'I wish to dance with you.'

There was just a hint of command to the statement—a tone she had not heard him use when they'd been together in the country.

'Very well,' she replied, surrendering, and took his arm to allow him to lead her to the floor. 'But be warned: I have never waltzed before and might not be very good at it.'

'You will be fine,' he said, in a soft tone that made her believe that just for a few minutes everything would be all right.

Then he pulled her into his arms and they began to dance.

After a moment's silence, he said, 'You did not say goodbye when you left Shropshire.'

'I departed rather suddenly,' she replied, making an effort to look past him, rather than into his eyes.

'And got engaged suddenly as well,' he said.

There was a hint of censure in his voice, as though he had a right to approve or disapprove the matter.

She held her head high, to show him she didn't care what he thought. 'My parents arranged it for me.'

'When I knew you, you seemed quite adamant that you would make your own way in the world,' he reminded her.

'My father presented a very convincing argument against that,' she said. 'One that I was unable to resist. It seems I am not as brave as I claimed to be.'

'You were quite strong enough to refuse me, as I remember,' he said in a mild voice.

'That was different,' she said, refusing to allow her hurt to show. 'What we had was a fleeting thing, not strong enough to last a lifetime. You'd have come to regret your decision, given time.'

'So you destroyed it to save me the trouble?' he said, with just a hint of bitterness. 'But that does not mean that you could not have left me a letter of farewell. You wrote so many words while we were together. Did you have none for me?'

'There was no time,' she repeated, trying not to think of how desolate he'd been because he had not been able to say farewell to Emma. 'And my parents would certainly not have allowed me to have paper, since they consider any writing at all as a sign of my mania.'

'Is that what you are calling it now?' he asked. 'Do you believe your writing is an aberration?'

'Father says there are doctors who will cure me of it if I do not take steps to curb the habit myself,' she admitted, then watched as his jaw tightened.

'You are speaking of an asylum?'

She could feel his arms tense as he held her.

'It was not necessary,' she said, feeling a wave of panic at the memory. 'My writing was a hobby— nothing more than that. Now that the second book is completed, my interest has waned.'

She thought of the manuscript, probably still sitting in the hide. Perhaps he would send it to her, once she was out of her parents' house. It might be nice to have it—just to remember a time when she had been free to express her thoughts. But she doubted her husband would be any happier about it than her parents had been.

'And what of your readers?' he asked. 'Might they not want more stories from you?'

'They shall just have to read something else,' she said with a sigh. 'I am sure it shall not be long until another book becomes the fashion. They will not be bothering me about it, in any case, for my parents have managed to quash all the rumours that were swirling about my first book. The author remains anonymous.'

'Hmm…' he said, his head giving a little jerk of surprise. Then he added, 'Please tell me it was not my opinion that put such ideas into your head.'

'Of course not,' she said hurriedly. 'It is not as if your view would matter more than anyone else's.'

'Of course not,' he said, just as hurriedly.

'It is just that the consensus seems to be that my aspirations were foolish. And when an offer of marriage presented itself…'

She could not help the tired sigh that escaped her when she thought of a lifetime with Mr Smollett.

'But it is not a love match?' Martin prompted.

She laughed. 'Did you think it possible for me to fall in love in such a short time?'

Although, of course, she had known Martin only a few days before developing a strong attraction to him. Perhaps it *would* be possible to develop a similar attraction to the man she was supposed to marry.

If only this one would go away, so she might forget him.

'And what of your work?' she asked, to change the subject. 'Are you still living with a completed manuscript and no plans to publish?'

'On the contrary. Our last discussion changed my mind on the subject. I have brought it with me to London and submitted it to the British Museum for review.' He clearly could not help smiling. 'They are quite impressed with the work, and we are discussing publication in the next year.'

'Oh, Martin,' she said, squeezing his hand and unable to help her excitement. 'I would most like to read it when it becomes available. Your paintings at least should be displayed. They are so lifelike.'

'You shall have the first copy,' he said, and favoured her with a look that all but stopped her heart. 'Your opinion means much to me.'

'I would like that,' she said—and then remembered that when such a book arrived she would have to explain to her husband what she was doing with it. But since he already assumed she liked birds he should have no suspicions about it. What harm could there be in something scholarly that was not frivolous, like *The Mad Monk of Montenero?*

For now, she would focus on the fact that Martin truly had changed for the better—and she had been the cause of it. The fact that it had come too late for them was not something that could be helped.

The music was ending and he took her arm, leading her towards a chair. 'It has been good to see you, Felicity,' he said softly.

'And you,' she replied, not wanting to let him go.

'And who is this gentleman?' her father asked, in a voice that sounded jovial but in her experience was anything but.

'Lord Woodley, may I present my father, Mr John Morgan?' Felicity said, stepping out of the way so the men could bow to each other. 'I met Lord Woodley in Shropshire,' she supplied, then added, 'He is heir to the Duke of Ashton.'

She was pleased to see her father start.

'We are honoured by your presence, my lord,' he said.

'When I heard that Felicity was marrying, I could not stay away.'

If her father was shocked by his use of her given name, he did not show it. Instead, he said, 'You must meet the happy man who has claimed her. Come with me. I am sure we shall find him in the card room.'

'Certainly,' Martin said, with a steely glint in his eye. 'I can hardly wait.'

And then the two of them strolled off together, leaving her alone.

Smollett was a toad. There was no other way to describe him.

Actually, there was. Given a little brandy, and

enough time, Martin would be able to think of any number of things he'd like to call the man—many of them directly to his face. When he'd realised that Martin had power, he'd been unctuously deferential, just as Morgan was. Both had seemed eager enough to use Felicity to gain a connection to him, but were quick to forget her now that the introduction had been made.

Neither of them noticed or cared that the poor girl was miserable, and that she would not have gone through with this sham of an engagement if she had not been threatened with something far worse.

The question was, had his presence made things worse or better? She had turned him down in Shropshire and given no indication that she would reconsider her answer if he asked again.

Some primal part of him rose up in irritation and announced that it did not matter. He was here to win her. If she did not like it now, she would soon see the error of this engagement and come back to him. Perhaps he should kidnap her and run for the border, like a character in one of her books.

But if she truly wanted to be single, a forced marriage to him would be no different from one to Smollett. Of course there were things he could offer that this interloper could not. But she had already told him that she didn't want them.

There was little he could do about the title that was coming to him. If they married she would end up as a duchess, whether she liked it or not.

But surely there were some advantages to having such power? She would be allowed eccentricities that ordinary women would not.

For a moment he imagined her books, with their authorship attributed to Lady Woodley, and how excited his mother would be by the fact. Felicity might not know it, but she was likely the only woman in England her mother thought favourably of.

She was also the only woman in England who was brave enough to stand up to the Duchess of Ashton. That alone was reason for him to marry her. Not as important as the love he felt for her, but a point in her favour all the same.

They belonged together, whether she saw it or not. And in just a few days, when his plan came to fruition, he would make his offer again and have her answer.

Chapter Twenty-Two

'Are you feeling all right, my dear?' her mother asked, staring across the breakfast table at her.

'I did not sleep well,' Felicity admitted, staring down into her chocolate and wishing it was something stronger.

'You said the same thing yesterday,' her mother said with a worried look.

In truth, she had barely slept since the ball, three days ago. The brief naps she'd taken had been plagued with fevered dreams of lovemaking with Martin, nightmares about their arguments and the bitter sweetness of their waltz together, when she should have been in the arms of another man.

He should never have been invited to the ball, for it had awakened those feelings that she was trying to lay to rest. The only saving grace in the experience was that his mother had sent her regrets, for she could imagine the sort of congratulations that lady might have offered on meeting Mr Smollett.

'Are you ill?' her mother prompted, still staring at her.

'Only tired,' she replied with a forced smile.

At the end of the table her father rustled his newspaper, as if to warn her that he would tolerate no more nonsense from her, then he said, 'If you are tired you can always return to your room and cease worrying your mother.'

She resisted the urge to make a rude face at the paper between them. What had she ever done to make him so impatient with her? And what reason had he ever given her to respect him?

For a moment, the strength of her emotions frightened her—for if she had felt love when she was with Martin, surely what she felt in this house was nothing more than loathing in response to the disrespect directed towards her.

She should have run when she'd had the chance, back in Shropshire. But run to whom? When she'd needed Martin he had been hiding in his house and she'd been left to face her parents alone.

That was not what one of her heroes would have done. But then, the men she created were perfect. They rose above their pasts rather than letting tragedy freeze them in place. And since she must now prepare herself for the cold and bitter reality of a marriage to Mr Smollett she had best forget about them—and Martin as well.

Suddenly there was a pounding on the front door. The banging of someone too impatient to bother with the knocker.

Her mother started nervously.

Her father closed his paper with another rustle and slapped it down on the table next to his plate, looking even more annoyed by this stranger than he had been with her.

From the hall she could hear Mr Smollett, demanding that he speak with her father immediately.

The family turned as one towards the door to the dining room as the housekeeper showed him in.

It was immediately clear that something was wrong. Her future husband was not wearing the smile of an eager suitor. He was staring at her with the same barely contained annoyance she was used to seeing from her father.

'Mr Smollett,' her mother said with a conciliatory smile. 'We had not expected a visit from you today. But it is always good to see you.'

'You think so, do you?' he said, shaking the newspaper he held in his hand. 'I suppose you did not mean to tell me about this until it was too late?'

'This…?' her mother said, staring at the folded paper. 'I have no idea…'

She looked to Felicity for an explanation, but all she could do was shrug in response.

He opened the paper, paging through it and folding it back with shaking hands before dropping it in front of her father. That man looked down at the exposed page, then erupted with a full-throated, 'Damn!'

Then he looked at Felicity, with the same angry expression that her betrothed was wearing.

'You must know that after this the betrothal cannot go forward,' Mr Smollett said with a disgusted look.

'But our daughter's honour…' her mother said weakly.

'If she means to be a public spectacle, it is clear that she has no care for it—and neither do I,' Mr Smollett said.

'I swear, sir, I have no idea what I have done,' Felicity said, looking from Smollett to her father and trying to control the unwarranted thrill she felt at the thought of being free.

'Then read it for yourself,' Mr Smollett said. 'No man will want you if you behave in such a way.'

Then he turned and stormed out of the house, slamming the door behind him.

Now it was her father's turn to visit his wrath upon her. 'Foolish girl!' he said, paging through his own copy of *The Times*. 'After all we have done to separate you from this nonsense…the sacrifices we've made to restore your reputation…still you proceed, unheeding, towards ruin. If we cannot find a way to repair this breach I will have you committed, just as I told you.'

'I tell you, Father, I cannot think what I have done to cause such a response,' she said.

'Then how do you explain *this*?' he demanded, thrusting the paper under her nose.

She pulled back and took it from him, scanning the page that had been folded open.

It was an advertisement announcing the publication of the sequel to *The Mad Monk* and encouraging people to order the book before the first printing sold out. And there, in large point type, was her name as its author.

She could not help smiling with pride. And then she realised that was not the response that was expected from her at all. She was supposed to be as appalled as her parents that her name had been associated with such a book.

After some struggle, she managed to contain her true emotions and looked to her father helplessly.

'I had nothing to do with this. I did not submit the manuscript for publication.'

'But you admit you wrote it?' he said.

'You know I did. I told you. It was a way to pass the time in Shropshire. But I had no idea…'

At least, she'd had none since leaving the country. Once arriving in London, she had given up hope.

'I thought you were lying to provoke me. I did not really believe you would defy me after I expressly forbade you from writing,' her father said, shaking his head in disgust. 'After we did everything in our power to see to it that you would not have the means to indulge your disgusting hobby?'

'It is not as easy to stop as you might think,' she said, and then knew that she'd misspoken. By the dark look on his face she had only proved his point that writing was a form of madness. 'But I swear I left the manuscript behind when you brought me home,' she added.

Which begged the question: how had it got here and into the hands of Mr Ransom, the publisher?

There was only one answer.

Martin.

She smiled, but only for a moment, not wanting to make her father any angrier than he already was.

'I see that smirk on your face,' he said, raising his fist as if ready to strike her. 'Go ahead! Laugh as your future walks out through the door. You will not remain under my roof one day longer, colouring the family with your madness. You can go to Bedlam for all I care.'

'Now, John…' her mother said, trying to calm him.

'If she does not want a proper marriage, then she should not expect to live here,' her father went on, warming to the subject. 'I will call the doctor and have her put away—just as I promised.'

She knew she should be frightened, for she could imagine what awaited her should he carry through on the threat. She had written about just such gothic torture for her heroine in the latest book. Instead, she rose from her seat so quickly that her chair tipped and crashed to the floor.

'You will not,' she said, backing away from him.

And then, before he could say another word, she turned and ran.

She was at the front door before he could get out of his chair. She opened it and rushed through it— into the arms of a man standing on the threshold.

'What—' she said. The breath had been forced from her body with the impact.

'Miss Morgan.' Martin's arms came around her to steady her, and she fought the urge to collapse against him. 'Let us go back into the house.'

She shook her head, thinking of her father and his final threat. 'I must get away from here,' she whispered urgently.

'We will leave together,' he promised. 'No matter what happens.'

Then he led her back to her parents.

She clung to his arm, digging her fingers into the wool of his tan coat. He was even more smartly dressed than he'd been at the ball, every bit the polished heir to a peer. His hessians shone so brightly that she was sure she could see her reflection in them.

She wondered at his appearance, and was surprised to find she missed the ridiculous coat he had worn to go birding. The man who had worn that had been her lover. Who was this elegant stranger who had promised to rescue her but was taking her back to her father?

Her father was standing just inside the dining room doorway, still simmering with rage at her attempt to flee.

Martin stood before him, unfazed, and said, 'Mr Morgan. I believe we spoke at the ball the other night.'

'Lord Woodley?'

Her father could not seem to decide between awe and irritation at this fresh invasion.

Martin ignored his hostility, smiling as if he was sure of his welcome here. 'I passed Felicity's former fiancé in the street just now. Since it appears that their union is not to be, I have come to pay court to your daughter.'

'You cannot be serious!' her mother blurted, near to tears. 'She is a public disgrace.'

'I will be the judge of that,' Martin said, staring at the pair of them with a cool superiority that Felicity had not seen before. Today, he looked every bit the Duke he would someday be. 'And I say she has done nothing so shocking that I will not have her.'

'Then you must not have read the papers,' her father said, flinching at the memory of what he had seen there.

'Read the papers?' Martin said with a laugh. 'It was I who composed the advertisement. I took the book to the publisher and the printer, as well,' he added. 'I also collected Miss Morgan's earnings from the previous book. And I will give them to her at such time as I am sure you will not simply take them away again. If she refuses me she will have quite enough money to survive without the help of any of us.'

'Refuses you?' her father said, clearly still thinking that he could control the situation. 'What sort of a damn fool do you take her for? She will say yes if she knows what's good for her.'

'She does not want to marry. When she was in Shropshire she was quite adamant on the subject,' he said, glancing at her and then back to her father.

They were both talking about her as if she was not there to decide for herself. If this was part of a heroic rescue then perhaps it was not as nice as she'd imagined it to be.

'If I could talk to the Marquess alone…' she said, before either of them could speak again.

'Of course,' her mother said, before her father could contradict her, seizing her husband's arm and pulling him back into the dining room.

'Somewhere more private…' Felicity said, glancing towards the front door.

'Go into the sitting room,' her mother called over her shoulder.

'And do not come out until you have come to your senses,' her father added.

Felicity escorted Martin out of the hall and into the parlour, then shut the door behind them, listening for a moment before turning to lean her back against it for support.

'What have you done?'

'The only thing I could have, under the circumstances,' he said, smiling at her. 'I have destroyed your engagement.'

'How…?' she said, unable to continue.

'I saw it in *The Times*,' he said. 'And I saw that it was announced before you'd even left for London. Since you were adamant on not marrying, I came to see what had changed your mind. And since you were obviously unhappy at the ball…'

'What made you think…?'

He held up a hand to stop her. 'I know you, Felicity. I know what you look like when you are happy.'

There was something in the way he said those words that made her knees weak, as she thought of all the times he had brought her to the ultimate joy. She smiled back at him, and he nodded in satisfaction.

He continued. 'I could see the misery in you as we danced. I knew this marriage was something that your father was forcing you into and you needed rescuing.'

'And you took that upon yourself?' she said, thinking of her novels and the men in them and the way they always took the initiative.

'You had mentioned your publisher, and declared your manuscript finished, so I simply united the two.'

'And what of Mr Smollett?'

He gave a dismissive shake of his head. 'I spoke to him in the card room at the ball. He is not the man for you.'

'He was here just before you. I suspect the retraction of his offer will be in tomorrow's paper,' she said with a smile and a shrug.

'I am aware of that. I was waiting outside your house to see if he would come in person to give you the news.' At this, Martin looked positively gleeful. 'And, really, the two of you do not suit at all. He struck me as the sort of man who would not abide a wife given to selling her fantasies on the open market.'

'In that you share an opinion,' she said, losing some of her enthusiasm.

'About that...' he said with a sheepish grin. 'Now that I have read your work, I think I owe you an apology.'

'You have read my book?' she said, shocked.

'Both of them,' he admitted.

'The sequel as well? But I never show my work to people before it is finished.'

'I was under the impression that it *was* finished,' he said. 'And since my mother had read it...'

'You let the Duchess read my book?' she said, her shock turning to horror.

'She insisted,' he said. 'When she realised that

you were the authoress of *The Mad Monk of Montenero* she would give me no peace until she had read the sequel.'

'She knew *The Mad Monk*?' she asked, surprised.

'She is obsessed with it. She's read it several times and was beside herself when she realised that she'd had the author so close at hand and not quizzed her on the next book. So I gave her the manuscript.'

'Did she like it?' Felicity asked, holding her breath.

'We both agree that it is even better than the first one.'

She sagged in relief.

'It is now safely in the hands of your friend Mr Ransom.' He paused. 'And here is where I took some liberties you might not approve of. I told Mr Ransom that I would bring you the profits from the sale of the first book…' he patted his pocket '…but I used my own money to pay for the printing of the second. If I was being too forward I will take you there now, so you can make whatever arrangements you wish to secure your future.'

'That was most kind of you,' she said carefully. 'And I will pay you back. But why did you bother? My problems are not yours.'

'Not as yet,' he said, clasping his hands behind his back and pacing the length of the room. 'But there is another matter that I wish to discuss.'

'And what would that be?' she asked, daring to hope again.

'Your reason for not marrying,' he said, staring at the floor. 'Is it a complete aversion to the institution? Or just a fear of the loss of your freedom to pursue your chosen vocation?'

'The latter,' she said.

'And love?' he said. 'What are your opinions on that?'

She felt a rush of the emotion just from looking at him. But it would not do to blurt the words out and burden him with them until she was sure of his intent.

'I believe it would be an important part of such a union,' she said cautiously. 'As I have told you before, I would not wish to marry someone who was not capable of feeling it for me.'

'And suppose that man did love you?' he said. 'Suppose he discovered that he loved you most desperately, and in a way he'd never felt before?'

'I would like that more than I can say,' she said gently. 'If it were the right man, of course.'

He looked up at her then, smiling. 'We are quite a pair, aren't we? Violently opposed to marriage, and yet here we are.'

'Where are we, exactly?' she asked, eager to hear him say it.

He unclasped his hands and walked over to her, reaching out to take her hands in his. 'I thought I could never love again,' he said, shaking his head as if amazed. 'But then I met you.'

'And your pledge to your wife? And to yourself...?' she said cautiously.

'It was the oath of a foolish young man,' he said. 'When Emma died I was broken. I thought I could never be whole again. And then you came into my life and put the pieces back together.'

She smiled, for she could not help it.

He continued. 'I did not think it was possible to have a love like I had with Emma again, and I was right.'

Her hopes fell. Just as she'd feared, she might never have his heart.

'But I see now that each love is different. What I felt for Emma was like a summer day that seemed endless. What I feel for you is the hope that one feels on the first day of spring, after surviving a long winter.'

'Winter might come again,' she said.

'It always does,' he agreed. 'But when it does I will not be lost in it, as I was. There is hope, Felicity, and you have given it to me.'

He was smiling at her in a way that warmed not just her blood, but her heart. Then he gathered her to him in a kiss that left no doubt as to his feelings for her.

Their lips parted, but he did not release her, holding her tight against him and letting the warmth and strength of his body shield her, wiping away the fears she'd had just moments ago.

'Marry me, Felicity,' he said in an urgent whisper. 'Come away with me right now. We will have a special licence in days and be wed before the week is out. Or we can go to Scotland and be married even sooner.'

'And you would allow your future duchess to write?' she asked, amazed.

'Didn't you realise after meeting my mother? A duchess can do whatever she wants. The rest of us are quite powerless to stop it.'

'I quite like the sound of that,' she said, smiling up at him.

'I thought you would,' he agreed, smiling back. 'And now I think it is time we said farewell to your parents.'

'Where are we going?' she asked.

'I have not thought that far ahead,' he said. 'But wherever it is, we will be going together.'

Then he sealed the promise with another kiss.

* * * * *

COMING SOON!

We really hope you enjoyed reading this book.
If you're looking for more romance
be sure to head to the shops when
new books are available on

Thursday 15th August

To see which titles are coming soon, please visit
millsandboon.co.uk/nextmonth

MILLS & BOON

MILLS & BOON®

Coming next month

CAPTIVATED BY HIS CONVENIENT DUCHESS
Lauri Robinson

'When do you plan on marrying her?'

'Tomorrow.'

'Tomorrow?'

'Yes, that's why I requested you here today. I'll need you as a witness at the wedding. Brunswick sent a message that she agreed to the marriage and is due to arrive before evening.'

Wesley lifted a brow, but a knock interrupted anything he was about to say.

'Come in,' Myles said, rising to his feet.

'Excuse me, sir,' Charles, their long-time and still overly spry butler said. 'There is a carriage coming up the driveway that appears to be out of control. I've sent Gus to the stables to get help, but I'm not sure what else to do.'

Myles wasn't sure what to do, either, other than rush outside and figure out what could be done. Wesley ran beside him, racing down the steps and watching the carriage careen around the last curve in the road and barrel forward. A woman was driving it, with a single bright blue feather flopping atop her hat like she'd struck a bird en route and one of its tail feathers had got stuck to her head. The horses didn't appear to be out of control, but she had to be out of her mind to drive them at such speeds in this weather.

Myles couldn't tell if it was with expertise or sheer determination, by the look on her face, that she brought the steaming horses to a stop so close to the front steps that both he and Wesley had to jump back to keep from getting hit.

'There's a man freezing to death inside the coach!' she shouted. 'He fell in the river! Hurry! Get him inside the house!'

Groomsmen from the stable were arriving two at a time, and Myles instructed them to get the man inside the house.

As Myles stepped back, giving the men room, Wesley caught sight of the coach occupants, then looked up at the woman driver, who was telling the grooms to be careful, but hurry.

'That's her, isn't it?' Wesley whispered.

'I believe so,' Myles admitted, as a chill that had nothing to do with the cold air coiled around his spine.

Wesley slapped his back. 'I wouldn't call that meek, brother. You ever rescued a hellcat before?'

Myles ignored his brother and turned his full attention on the woman driver as the other men carried the man towards the house. Maybe all of his thoroughness hadn't been quite thorough enough. She wasn't meek. Nor was she unattractive, as he'd also been told, granted that had been by Brunswick when Myles had said he was interested in her, not Brunswick's daughters. Even with her hat askew and her hair dripping wet, the fineness of her features was enough to steal a man's breath.

Continue reading
CAPTIVATED BY HIS CONVENIENT DUCHESS
Lauri Robinson

Available next month
millsandboon.co.uk